LIKE JAGGED TEETH

BETTY ROCKSTEADY

PMMP

Perpetual Motion Machine Publishing
Cibolo, Texas

Like Jagged Teeth
Copyright © Betty Rocksteady 2017

ISBN: 978-1-943720-21-7

www.PerpetualPublishing.com

Cover Art by Betty Rocksteady
www.bettyrocksteady.com

ALSO BY BETTY ROCKSTEADY

Arachnophile

CHAPTER 1

THEY WERE DEFINITELY following her.

The whole night had been a mistake. Jacalyn never should have bothered with the party. She should have stayed home and helped Mom look after Nanny, but she was *never* invited out anymore and she couldn't stand looking at that sad, wrinkled face every night of her life. So she went to the party, and she sat on the outskirts, picking at her nails and staring at her phone, until she realized it had been nearly an hour since she had spoken a word to anyone. How the hell did you make friends as an adult, anyway? What a waste of time. So she called a cab, but waiting outside alone made her all teary-eyed. She was tired and she was uncomfortable and she decided to walk.

And that was her real mistake.

She couldn't go much faster. Her heels pinched and a blister was forming where her foot rubbed against the plastic. Why hadn't she had worn something more practical? She wished she could run. The street was too dark and it was getting too cold, freezing for a summer night. She should have stayed with her friends. She should have just waited for the cab, no matter how long it was taking, but she didn't, and now here she was and they were definitely following her.

Two guys, in their 30s at least, too old to be playing these kinds of games. She resisted looking back over her shoulder. From the sound of their voices, she knew they were getting closer. Looking back would only egg them on. They kept shouting at her and she tried to block them out, block out their comments about her short skirt and chubby legs. They were drunk, but that didn't mean they were dangerous. They might just be obnoxious. But she was scared, oh, she was scared, and she just wanted to get home.

She unzipped her purse, quiet as she could, and fumbled out her phone. The battery was low, 3%, and why the fuck hadn't she charged it all the way before she left? Because this wasn't supposed to happen. Sarah *said* she was going to drive Jacalyn home, but then Sarah wanted to stay at the party and Jacalyn wasn't having fun anymore. Why couldn't stop making such stupid decisions?

"Hey, cutie, where you goin' in such a hurry? You shouldn't be walking alone, why don't ya let us walk with you? Wanna make sure ya get home safe."

Jacalyn glanced back, she couldn't help it, only for a second. Her heart jumped to her throat. There was only half a block between them, but that wasn't the worst thing. The hunched posture of the man on the left was hiding something, writhing beneath his shirt. And was he wearing a mask? Distorted features crowded his face, dripping and liquid. The other man grinned yellow and it seemed to split his face in two.

She turned away and walked faster, putting more distance between them. God, would this walk never end? Still blocks to go and then she would have to juggle her keys in front of her sleeping house while they got closer.

Her shoes rubbed against her new blister, getting more painful with each step. Don't look back. Keep going. Ignore the pain. Fuck. Fuck. Fuck. She didn't want these creeps to know where she lived. Jacalyn's sweaty hand tightened around her phone. She couldn't very well call the police. They hadn't actually done anything . . . yet. Fuck.

A car growled behind her, headlights illuminating the sidewalk ahead. A horn honked three times. She jumped a little and walked faster.

"Hey, old man, isn't it past your bedtime?"

The car caught up with her and slowed down, beeping its horn again. Jacalyn blinked away tears. Why couldn't they just leave her alone? Why couldn't everyone just leave her alone?

"Jacalyn," a familiar voice purred. "Get in, I'll give you a lift."

She turned in slow motion. The moon wavered in front of her eyes. A low, dark car loomed in front of her. The driver leaned out his window, smiling kindly at her, wrinkles crinkled around his eyes. The world went double, the last few vodka shots finally kicking in, and her knees trembled.

"Poppa?"

"Come on, babygirl, get in." A click as he unlocked the passenger seat. It was impossible. Her memories fought to catch up, to line themselves up with the reality in front of her. Everything else faded away, the boys, the whole shitty evening, the dark slice of moon in front of her.

"Poppa, you're dead."

BETTY ROCKSTEADY

"It's a long story, baby, I'll get you all caught up. Get in."

The men were catching up now. "Hey, is this old geezer bothering you?" A sound of static. Jacalyn's head spun. She stared into the sparkling eyes of her dead grandfather. She opened the car door and climbed in. Poppa clicked the button and locked the door again, just as the men caught up. He smiled at her. Then he drove, leaving them behind like a dream.

The car was warm, stuffy, just how Poppa liked it. It was hard to breathe in a car with the heat up so high. She liked to have fresh air running through. Dizzily, she thumbed the button for the window, but it remained shut tight.

"I need to get that fixed," her grandfather said. He stared straight ahead, at the road, deep in concentration. He always hated driving at night, especially as he got older. She looked at his face in profile. His sharp nose, hair swept back, still thick and dark grey with only a tiny bald spot. A light stubble peppered his cheeks and chin. Faded, comfortable plaid draped his body, dressed too warm for the summer evening. He had died in the autumn. "Do you want to go straight home, or are you coming back to my apartment for a while?"

"Poppa, I—" The stale air clouded her thinking. It was too hard to breathe. All the blood had left her head. She tugged her skirt toward her knees and saw that her hands were shaking. Shock? Was this what shock felt like? Her mind raced to catch up, but the drinks plus the air plus Poppa . . . her head spun. "Poppa, you've been . . . I haven't . . . "

He took his eyes from the road briefly to look at her. His hand reached over to pat her naked knee, squeezed it comfortingly. "It's a lot to take in, baby-doll, I know. But obviously, I'm not dead." His laugh was hearty and soothed her heart. Tears sprang to her eyes.

"Where have you been? I don't understand."

"We're almost at your house, do you want me to drop you off? We can talk later."

"No! Don't make me go home yet!" This could all seem like a dream in moments. "Where . . . where are you staying? Are you with Nanny still—I . . . "

"No. It's a long story. Does that mean you want to come back to my apartment with me? It's a two bedroom, you can stay for the night if you want! I'll make you breakfast in the morning and we can hash all this out."

"I . . . I should call Mom. Does Mom know?"

"No." His voice went harsh, hoarse. Her heart thudded. He sounded angry. She didn't want to make him angry. "Don't call your mother. There's plenty of time for all this in the morning. It's a bit of a drive, so why don't you just relax? It's too much to talk about while I'm trying to pay attention to the roads. This bloody darkness, I can't see a damn thing."

"Yeah . . . yeah, that's fine." She stared at him. It was impossible, but it was amazing. Her Poppa was back. There was so much to tell him about! She had so many questions. But he was right, now wasn't the time to start up with all this. Not while she was still drunk, and with shock making her sleepy. The hum of the car made her eyes heavy. The scent of her grandfather's cologne swam through her head.

With blurry eyes, she watched her home roll slowly past. Her mom would be long asleep, anyway. She didn't wait up for her anymore. Calling her in the middle of the night to tell her that Poppa was alive would hardly be reassuring. He must have a good reason for keeping all this a secret.

Something tugged at her brain, something dark and clawed, but the smell of cologne and the heat buried it. She couldn't think about it now. She couldn't think about anything now. A reluctant yawn escaped, refusing to be stifled. God, how could she be tired after all this?

"You sound pretty sleepy there, sweetie. Why don't you go ahead and close your eyes? I'll wake you up when we get back to my place. It's a bit of a drive."

"Okay, Poppa." He wavered in front of her eyes, just slightly. Maybe this was all a dream, but it was a nice one. She had her Poppa back. There was so much to tell him. So much he would be proud of. So much he could help her with. She had missed him every single day. There was that tugging in the back of her mind again, but she pushed it away. She was too tired, far too tired to think about that now.

She reached out instead. His hands were clenched on the wheel, so she touched his shoulder. Felt the fuzzy material rub against his soft old man muscles. A smile twitched at the corner of his lips.

"I love you, Poppa."

"I love you too, sweetie."

His eyes looked too dark for a moment, just as hers blinked closed, and then she was asleep.

CHAPTER 2

THERE WAS SOMETHING huge and dark and screaming behind her. Gnarled hands reached from the walls, twisting her skin, leaving leaking pustules wherever they touched. The hallways grew narrower. Breath was heavy on the back of her neck. A door ripped open and broken stairs like jagged teeth loomed in front of her. Something penetrated her back, spearing her like a butterfly. She twisted and fell, down thousands of stairs, her delicate bones shattering and splintering until she was in pieces on the floor. And it was still coming. It was always coming.

She was tangled in unfamiliar blankets, enveloped in the darkness of an unknown room. Her breath came fast and hard, like she had been running. Her throat was dry, as if she had been talking too loud for too long. Or screaming.

Where was she? The dream feeling lingered. The events of last night were impossible. Maybe those creeps had gotten her after all and she had hit her head. Poppa couldn't really be alive. Could he? It was too dark to make sense out of where she was, her brain was thick and fuzzy and she was afraid to call out.

BETTY ROCKSTEADY

She was surrounded by shadow. The shapes peeking out from the darkness were cryptic. This was not her room. Her heart thudded in her chest, too loud, too hard. She pitched off blankets, thick and itchy against her clammy skin.

Movement. Creaks and groans as the room shifted. Something smelled bad, rotten. Her eyes took too long to adjust to the dark. Light. She needed light.

She could just make out the shape of a lamp next to the bed. Her skin prickled and she was suddenly certain someone was in the room with her, and their lascivious eyes crept over her skin as she reached for the lamp. It was farther away than it looked. She shuffled across the bed, balanced on the edge of it, afraid to put her feet on the floor.

Her hands were useless and clumsy. She fumbled against the lamp as she searched for the switch. It felt sticky. Finally, she found the switch and clicked the light on.

The illumination was a dull yellow and barely made a dent on the darkness. She could hardly see her own shaking hands. The rest of the room was lost in inky shadow. The curtains next to her bed were drawn tightly shut, so she pulled them open. It was still night. It felt like she had been asleep forever, but the moon was large and orange in the sky. Had it been a full moon earlier? She couldn't remember. A chill ran up her spine, freezing her entire body. Her feet were like shards of ice. She drew the heavy blanket back around her shoulders, reluctantly. The itchy wool fibers tickled against her.

Was this really Poppa's apartment?

From her spot on the bed, she couldn't see much, but everything she saw looked old, disused. The room could have been decorated in the '60s. The wallpaper was peeling, yellow, faded bits of paisley dripping from the walls. Mossy carpet covered the floor, matted and stained. She couldn't see much else with the limited illumination of the lamp. There must be a switch for the overhead light, but the idea of plunging her bare feet into that carpet was sickening.

She realized she was nearly naked, had been put to bed in her underwear. Poppa would never have undressed her, she had to be forgetting something. How had he gotten her into the apartment without waking her up? She didn't even know where this apartment *was*.

She peered out the window. The building stretched endlessly down; the ground miles away. A high-rise apartment, in this city? Strange, but there could be a couple she wasn't aware of. Nerves tickled in her stomach. The ground was so far away. It didn't look right. It gently rose and fell in tandem with her breath. Unidentifiable shadows loomed just out of sight, something about them bringing back the panic of her dream. She let the curtains fall. She didn't want to look anymore.

She needed to talk to Poppa.

She grabbed the lamp and was dismayed to see that the extension cord didn't stretch very far. If she wanted light, she would have to walk blindly across the room, feeling grimy wallpaper beneath her fingers as she navigated, looking for a switch. But first she would walk on that awful carpet. She couldn't bring herself to do it. The shadows made her nervous. They seemed threatening, and it still felt like something was looking at her. It was silly. She wasn't a kid anymore. She wasn't afraid of the dark.

She needed to get up, look around the room, turn the light on, find the door. She wanted her clothes. She wanted her phone. Her charger was at home, but hopefully there was a little juice left. Enough to text Mom at least, tell her she was okay, that she had stayed at a friend's house or something, if Poppa didn't want her to know. But she stayed rooted to her spot on the bed. It didn't feel safe getting up in this strange place, in the dead of the night.

Jacalyn pulled the blanket tightly around herself. She still felt cold.

It was just that it was unfamiliar. And dark. Nothing was wrong.

She lay back down. The bed was hard and uncomfortable. The blanket didn't cover her right. Close your eyes, she told herself. It's gotta be daytime soon, and then you can talk to Poppa and find out what's going on.

She left the light on but didn't close her eyes. She could never fall asleep again. Not tonight. There was no way. She lay stiff as a board, afraid to move or roll over. How long before dawn?

There was a rhythmic ticking, so there had to be a clock here somewhere. Or was that the clicking of teeth? She could picture it all too well, her grandfather sitting behind those shadows, his thin frame crunched under a chair and his teeth in his hand, clicking and clicking rhythmically while his empty mouth smiled wide and she could practically see it and her breath came raspy and terrified and she could not sleep she would not . . .

but . . .

she did.

CHAPTER 3

SHE WOKE TO the scent of bacon frying and the rattle of pots and pans. Pale light streamed through the window and everything was fine. The bitter aroma of strong coffee wafted into the room, making her stomach churn. Anxiety tightened her chest. She should feel grateful—her Poppa was back, somehow, and she should be thrilled, but she just felt strange. She had slept too long and it made her head heavy and confused. The blanket was itchy against her bare flesh. What time was it? Her phone was not at the bedside table.

The light that streamed in the window lit up the entire room, but she couldn't see where Poppa had put her clothes. She wrapped the orange blanket around her body like a towel but still felt exposed.

The room was strange; familiar but wrong. It reminded her of Poppa's old house, and his spare room where she stayed during sleepovers, but everything was slightly askew. Well, of course it was. She was being silly. Putting the same furniture in a different apartment was bound to look different but . . . could this really be the same furniture? Her head was too fuzzy to catch up. She was sure Nanny had kept this stuff after Poppa died. But . . .

BETTY ROCKSTEADY

There was the chair that she and Poppa had curled up in to read—fat and brown and cozy. It took up too much room, bracketed on either side with overflowing bookshelves. The blanket drooped from her frame as she examined the books, unsteady on her feet. She must have had too much to drink last night. She never would have done that if she knew where she was going to end up. She only remembered having a few beers, a couple of shots, but everything felt so strange and liquid, like she was swimming through the room.

The books weren't what she expected. Not Poppa's usual fare. She found some of the collections of short fiction and fairy tales she had read as a child, but they were interspersed with books she didn't recognize. Poppa's books? No titles on the spines. She pulled one out, thick and dusty. She flipped a few pages and found it impossible to read. The writing was too small. Just looking at it intensified her headache. In the middle there were pages of diagrams detailing complex sexual positions, and Jacalyn felt her cheeks redden. She was snooping. She slid it back in the shelf and noticed a book she did recognize. It was the book she had lent Poppa when she had been going through her teen witch phase. Her grandparents, while not exactly old fashioned, had been a bit alarmed. They wanted to know the ins and outs of what she was getting involved in. But hadn't she taken this home after he had read it?

She pulled it out and flipped through the pages at random, still a bit shaken from the explicit pictures in the last one. A page of household correspondences—basil for luck, salt for protection. She had explained to Poppa a few of those correspondences, and he had found them fascinating, finally warming up to her new interest. She smiled at the memory, but only for a moment. It had all proved useless, hadn't it? It hadn't helped her at all. It was hard to have faith when the world sucked so much. She shoved the book back into place. Dishes clanged, bringing her back to the present situation.

Her head cleared a little and the nervousness gave way to excitement, a scary kind of excitement. What was she doing looking at books? She had to get dressed. She finally had a chance to talk to her Poppa again, to explain . . . to catch up. To tell him what she had done with her life. Even amidst the sick and blurry memories, she felt an overwhelming gratitude to have this chance again.

The chest of drawers near the bed must have her clothes and purse, and she rustled through them. Nothing here was hers. The drawers were mostly empty, filled with stained handkerchiefs, strange odds and ends. Greasy bars of soap. Maybe the closet, then.

The wooden doors were old and fragile. Jacalyn felt nervous to open them. She could just ask Poppa where her things were, but the idea of going out into that unknown apartment with just the blanket draped around her underwear felt wrong. Vulnerable. There must be something in here for her to wear.

The closet was stuffed with clothes. It smelled like Nanny. In fact, it looked exactly like the closet Nanny had in her spare room. Nanny never threw anything away. She had clothes all the way back to her teen years. Jacalyn had loved sifting through them and playing dress up. This closet was packed so tight it was hard to tug anything out, but she recognized a few items. There was the teal pantsuit Nanny would wear to bingo. An ancient floral nightgown, and behind that, an oily pair of leather pants.

"Jacalyn!" Poppa's voice boomed. He knocked a rat-a-tat-tat against the door, making her jump. "Breakfast is ready." His voice was warm and comforting as it wound its way into her heart.

"I'm just . . . do you have my clothes out there?"

"Just wear something of your grandmother's. There should be some pajamas in there that fit you. Hurry up, though, you don't want your breakfast to get cold." His slippers padded against the floor as he shuffled away.

The wallpaper shifted in her periphery. Dizzy. How much had she drank? She cursed herself for being so stupid. Imagine, the amazing opportunity to talk to her grandfather again and she had spoiled it by ruining her head beforehand.

She reached in again and was embarrassed to pull out a skimpy set of red lingerie. She pushed it aside and this time her hand landed on a floor-length nightgown straight out of the 1900s. She didn't recognize it, but it looked like it would fit and she pulled it on over her underwear. She wished she could wash her face and brush her teeth before going out to talk to Poppa. Everything about her felt slimy and unclean. There was a mirror on the wall and she swiped greasy hair back from her face. There was something red and sticky on the pajamas. It didn't matter. Something tried to click in her brain but she pushed it aside. She had a headache. She was tired. Everything would make sense soon, she was sure of it. Her chest tightened a warning, but she ignored it and opened the door.

CHAPTER 4

SHE STEPPED INTO a narrow hallway. The walls brushed her elbows, waking up an old claustrophobia. A cluster of photographs hung at strange angles. She thought they looked familiar, but between her fitful sleep and the intruding smell of breakfast, she was too nauseated to pay much attention. She did notice one picture that surely didn't belong here, Nanny thin and fragile in her sick bed, glaring at Jacalyn. She didn't pause to make sense of it, just brushed sweat from her brow and stumbled towards the sounds and smells of cooking.

Poppa waited in the kitchen, as if he had never been gone at all. He plated the crisp bacon and runny eggs next to fat undercooked sausage, his favorite breakfast. The wrinkles around his eyes folded as he smiled at her, but his eyes looked dull. Dead. A nagging memory kicked its way through the mist in her brain and her stomach churned again.

"I have to go to the bathroom." She didn't feel right. She should be happy. She should . . . she should say something else, but she was queasy and ready to vomit.

Poppa crinkled an eyebrow. "Next door down the hall, but hurry up, will you? I'm anxious to catch up." His voice was deep and throaty. A flash of guilt. She should be running into his arms but instead she stumbled to the bathroom and threw up in the toilet.

She hung her head, heaving and letting loose everything in her stomach. Her head floated, her arms shook. Feverish. Maybe she was coming down with the flu. She could hear Poppa muttering to himself in the kitchen. He must be so disappointed. This wouldn't have been what he expected. God, she was 24, and that was far too old to be getting drunk enough that she was sick the next day. It felt like she had already wasted most of the day sleeping, although she had no way of knowing the time.

Finally, she was able to lift herself on trembling knees. She slicked back greasy locks of hair. She flushed the toilet. The scent of her bile made her stomach contract all over again. It was a weak flush. Poppa's house always had a weak flush. Her own house had a good toilet, thank god, but Poppa had refused to replace the bathroom fixtures at his own house, even after updating countless other things about the place. She had sworn to herself that at her own home, when she grew up, toilet pressure would be a priority. And shower pressure. She glanced at the tub. She had the urge to turn the shower on and confirm her suspicions, but Poppa was waiting.

There was a film of blood in the bottom of the tub. Her heart beat in her ears. Was Poppa sick? He hadn't been . . . before . . . No. Her head was too cloudy. She went to the sink and washed her hands with a sliver of soap, rinsed in the thin trickle of water.

Her face looked far away in the reflection. She didn't feel like herself. Not at all. She never got this hung-over. She wobbled back to the kitchen. Poppa sat at the table, already halfway through his meal.

She sat, urging her stomach to remain as it was. Urging herself not to vomit again. She pulled at the sleeves of her pajamas. They didn't fit. Nanny's arms were much shorter than hers.

Poppa's looked at her across the table, warm brown eyes smiling. "It's so good to see you, Jacalyn."

It had been a long time. Looking into his eyes broke something inside her and she stumbled across the kitchen, nearly knocking her chair over. She threw her arms around him.

"Poppa!" She buried her face in his shoulder. "God, I missed you so much. I'm so sorry . . . sorry for . . . " but the words wouldn't come and beneath his musky scent there was . . . something else. Something rotten. He *must* be getting sick.

But he laughed and stroked her greasy hair. "I'm happy to see you too, sweetie, but really, sit. You need to eat. There's coffee brewing too."

The coffee smelled thin and bitter, but she thought she could get a bit down. Maybe it would knock some sense into her. The floor was sticky beneath her bare feet. She recognized the cup she chose from the cupboard. The handle was chipped, but the floral pattern was Nanny's favorite. But Nanny still had her set, didn't she? None of this made sense.

Jacalyn finally sat across from him. Her eggs had congealed to her plate. "This is all so surreal. Where have you been all this time? What . . . does anyone else know you're still alive? Where is this apartment? I don't even remember coming in last night! Are we still in the city?"

He laughed, finishing the last bit of sausage on his

plate. "So many questions. Eat your breakfast, we have lots of time to talk." He unfolded the newspaper and turned to the comics. He produced a pen and studied the crossword. A warmth flooded Jacalyn's chest. They had always done the crossword together. He had taught her how to do them. She felt the urge to scooch her chair up closer to his, but he peered over the newspaper at her and his eyes were hard.

"Jacalyn, you don't look well. Eat."

She stared at her plate. It was dirty. Nanny had always done the washing up, so now that Poppa was alone . . . but it didn't make sense. Why was he alone? Why wasn't he at home with Nanny? But Nanny lived with her and Mom now, because Nanny was sick. "Poppa."

He slammed a hand down on the newspaper, a dull thud against the table. His face went red and she shrank back. God, she hated making him angry. It didn't happen a lot, but when it did, it was sudden and all consuming.

"Jacalyn, eat your breakfast. There's plenty of time to talk later. I went through the trouble of making it, aren't you going to eat? It's been so long since we had a nice breakfast together."

"Sorry, Poppa, of course. It's good!" She forced a smile for him. An old guilt nagged at her chest. It was hard to be good enough sometimes. She was never as grateful as she should be.

The eggs looked bad. They had been left out too long. She salted them anyway. She sliced the sausage with her fork and red poured out of it. Her stomach turned over, but she ate the piece, chugging coffee quickly to chase it. It didn't taste right. Rubbery. Too chewy. The bacon was a little better, burnt but edible.

LIKE JAGGED TEETH

She watched Poppa, but he never looked up, consumed in the newspaper, making little marks in tiny squares. She kept hoping he would ask her opinion on one of the hints but he didn't. She ate quietly, not wanting to set him off again. She felt small and unhappy trying to choke down her meal. The eggs were impossible, even looking at them made her feel sick again. The toast was dry, but she was able to swallow it, and finally she finished her coffee. It had gone cold quickly. The whole mess made an uncomfortable lump in the pit of her stomach. She pushed the plate away, unable to look at it any longer.

Poppa looked over the newspaper at her finally. The disapproval in his eyes made her shuffle in her seat. This didn't feel right. None of this felt right. She couldn't meet his eyes, so she looked at the walls, hunting for a clock. She didn't even know if it was morning or afternoon. Either way, Mom would be worried; it was just a matter of how worried. There had been times Jacalyn had stayed out all night at a friend's place, but she always called or texted as soon as she knew where she was staying.

There was no clock anywhere. "What time is it?"

Poppa took her plate, flopping the newspaper on the table. He scraped it over the garbage, murmuring about the waste of food. "Have somewhere better to be?" There was humor in his voice, but there was also an edge to it.

"No, that's not it, not at all! I want to talk to you. There's so much . . . I have so much to tell you." Nothing was coming out right. Jacalyn felt dizzy. Even sitting upright in the chair was difficult. "Mom will just be worried. And Nanny. Where are my things? I want to call her."

"I put your things in the wash. They smelled of smoke and alcohol." His eyes were hard, but then his face softened in a smile. "Do you remember that time I caught you smoking out back? Thirteen or fourteen, weren't you? Left the door unlatched."

"Poppa . . ."

He chucked to himself. "I was giving you the old talking to and the dog snuck out the door. The stupid mutt ran out into the street and got her guts splattered all over the place. Musta been a big truck! By the time we got to her, she was just a mass of twitching organs." Poppa's eyes crinkled in amusement, smiling encouragingly at her. Her stomach clenched again.

"Can I use your phone?" Her voice sounded miles away.

Poppa shook his head. "I don't have one."

Jacalyn was sure she had seen one somewhere, but she was getting dizzy. It was hard to think of the right words. It was easier to stay quiet.

"I'll let your mom know where you are. Don't worry. I have to scoot out for a bit anyway, get my errands done. We can talk when I get home." He started to leave the room, and now Jacalyn did stand, on shaky feet.

"Don't go." Panic lit up her chest and clenched and wouldn't let go.

"Don't worry, I won't be long. Sit." He looked at her kindly. "Maybe you can finish the crossword puzzle for me." He disappeared out the kitchen door.

The light danced yellow. The kitchen spun in mad circles. Jacalyn reached for the paper but the lines and rows of letters wriggled and set off fireworks in her temples. Her head swayed atop her brittle neck.

LIKE JAGGED TEETH

She was so tired. Too tired. Poppa would wake her when he got home. She just needed to close her eyes for a minute.

As she drifted off she noticed that none of the words in the crossword had been filled in.

CHAPTER 5

SHE WOKE UP slowly, eyes heavy, blinking. Her face was pasted to the newspaper with drool. She peeled it off. Where was she? What time was it? The apartment was silent but for a faint buzzing coming from . . . somewhere.

The kitchen was too warm. Her skin felt slimy and she needed a shower. "Poppa?" Her voice echoed in the hallway and something about that empty tone made her feel nervous. Had he really left her alone here?

She hadn't noticed the phone before. It was on the wall beside her, huge and black and old fashioned. A spin dial. It had been a long time since she had seen one of those. Mom must be intensely worried by now, unless she was in on all this and knew what was going on. Jacalyn's thoughts fluttered by in her head, just out of reach. She just knew she wanted to talk to Mom, hear her comforting voice.

Standing up was difficult, so she did it slowly and leaned against the wall. The receiver was heavy in her hand. Sticky. Malignant. She didn't want to touch it. There was no dial tone, only static, but her hands reached out regardless, floated away from her body, out of her control. Her fingers fumbled in the dials.

LIKE JAGGED TEETH

She dialled wrong, dialled her old home number, from before they moved. She pushed down on the button to hang up, but it didn't make a difference. There was only static anyway. Tears came to her eyes and she didn't know why, just brushed them away.

There was a mumble beneath the static. Words. A lullaby. Her grandfather's voice. Her stomach moved. It felt like worms were writhing around down there. She remembered this song. Remembered it from when she was sick and tired and he would lay next to her and stroke her hair and sing.

She placed the phone back in its cradle. Lifted it again and this time there was nothing at all.

Her eyes were sandy. She blinked them a few more times. How long before Poppa would be back? What time *was* it? God, she felt like she had been stumbling around here for hours. She had to work tomorrow. She couldn't stay. As much as she wanted to know what was going on with Poppa, if he didn't get back soon she would have to leave. She could leave him a note. Something. She wanted to talk to her mother most of all—if anyone knew what was going on, it was her. Or Nanny. If Poppa were still alive, she would know, wouldn't she? Her health was so frail that Jacalyn couldn't imagine bringing this up with her.

A black rage snaked through her heart. This wasn't fair—to spring this on her and just disappear again. Why hadn't Poppa stayed? What could he possibly have to attend to that was more important than this? As quickly as it had started, the rage died. Maybe if she hadn't been so drunk last night, passed out, and then slept half the day away, it would all make sense by now. She had to take some of the responsibility herself. She should be feeling grateful and instead she was just being the same brat she had always been. Regret tightened her chest.

She couldn't sit at the table forever but she didn't want to snoop around. She wasn't like that anymore. Her throat was dry as sand. She needed a drink. He wouldn't mind that. She let the water in the tap run, but minutes passed and it never got better than murky looking. The fridge contained only that awful tomato juice Poppa liked. And wine. Homemade wine. She would just have to stay thirsty. Maybe he had gone out for groceries. When she was little and sick he had always brought her ginger ale.

The panicked feeling of wasted time caught up with her. Although it surely had been only minutes since she woke up, the quality of light coming into the kitchen had changed from daylight to dusk. Had she been stumbling around here longer than she thought? God, it shouldn't be getting dark already. She had been sleeping all day. The guilt pulled her chest tighter. She wanted to stay, she wanted to see Poppa, she desperately wanted to know what was going on but she couldn't stay here all night. She had to get home. Time was slipping through her fingers.

She staggered out into the hallway. She needed to find her purse. The pajamas clung to her, so itchy now, crawling over her skin. She needed to find her own clothes. She needed to go home, see her mom, sleep in her own bed. Everything was strange and heavy here.

The hallway was unfamiliar. Hadn't she come this way earlier? It was different now. All the doors were closed and Jacalyn couldn't remember which one led to her room. From the door at the end of the hall, she could hear movement. "Poppa?"

LIKE JAGGED TEETH

Her footsteps echoed in the hallway. She stood outside the door. There were voices, but they were distant. Muffled. She could hear raspy breathing. She placed her hand on the doorknob. She wanted to call to Poppa again, but her voice died in her throat. The doorknob felt wrong. Too warm. Too soft. She looked down at her hand and the anxiety in her chest turned into a vicious thrum. No. Not this door. Not now. She backed away.

Another doorknob jabbed into the small of her back and she turned and opened it quickly and slid inside. It was dark. She passed her hand along the wall, fumbling for a switch. Her hand brushed something that crumbled and died, and then the lights came on.

It was the room she had slept in. She released a breath she didn't know she was holding. This room felt safe.

꩜

Her things weren't under the bed. They weren't on the floor. They weren't on any of the bookshelves or the chair or the nightstand. Jacalyn's eyelid twitched. She wanted to go home. The mystery of this whole thing had dulled. It was awful of her to be so impatient to leave. It wasn't fair. This should have been much more important, but it was getting so dark outside. She didn't feel right being here any longer. Why had Poppa left her alone? Where the hell were her things? The pajamas she was wearing were tight and uncomfortable, straining at the seams. Even the things she had worn to the bar last night—tight skirt and buttoned blouse—would be more comfortable than this.

The feeling in her stomach kept nibbling away. Well, if she couldn't find her things, she could still leave. There had to be something she could wear outside at the very least—pajamas and barefoot wouldn't get her home but maybe if she could find something else she could go downstairs and find a phone at least. Fuck it. Leave her things here. Even Poppa couldn't expect her to stay here another night. She had school in the morning, and a shift at work tomorrow night.

She had wanted to tell him about school. She had finally taken the medical secretary course, and she was going to be finished in just weeks, starting her job placement. He would be proud. He had always had faith in her that she would make it, that she could do better for herself. She wished again she had a chance to talk to him, but now that she knew he was alive, there would be more time for that in the future. The idea of having a future with Poppa in it again was incredible, made her ashamed at the frustration she had been feeling.

The moon rose slowly, peered through the small window in her room. She was starting to think of this spare room as her own room already. It was certainly more comfortable to her than the rest of the apartment. She had to get a move on. Time was passing way too fast.

The closet door opened with a snap. The clothes were tightly packed, most of them covered in plastic, slippery and sticky in her grasp. She could have sworn earlier they had just been hanging there, but that was impossible. What, had Poppa just come in and covered them while she had been sleeping? She tried to tug out a few of the hangers to see if anything was wearable. She felt guilty even trying. It was like stealing, wasn't it? But she couldn't stay here forever, and she certainly couldn't wear the pajamas outside. Nanny wouldn't mind—did Nanny even know these clothes were here? A sharp pain shot through Jacalyn's head and she pushed the thought aside.

None of the clothes would come out. They were wedged tightly and no matter how she tugged and pulled she couldn't budge them more than an inch or two. "Fuck," she muttered, and her cheeks went pink at the sound of her own voice cursing in Poppa's apartment. She never cursed around him.

There were shoes on the floor of the closet. At least that would be a start. She crouched to examine them, all stilettos, much higher than her own modest heels. God, why didn't she just look in the living room? That was probably where her stuff was. It's not like Poppa was hiding it on purpose. But looking around his apartment without him wouldn't be right.

Behind the clothes, there was a door.

The appearance of the plain little door delighted her. She had always loved secrets like this. In Poppa's old house there had been a hidden door beneath the stairs. He had cleaned it out for her and put a few little shelves inside. She kept all her best things there. Books. Journals. Seashells. It had been one of her favorite places in the whole house. He often hid little treats and surprises in there for her to discover.

This door looked exactly like that one, only here it was, hidden behind the clothes, peeking out between shoes. She ducked underneath the plastic and grabbed the knob. She could almost imagine that when she opened it, within would be her own secret place.

BETTY ROCKSTEADY

Instead there was a dry, dusty smell, and a darkness that seeped out around her. The whole closet grew darker when she opened it. At first, she couldn't see anything at all when she peered inside, but then a bright blue shape came into view, near the back, an arm's length away. Her purse?

Maybe he had hidden a surprise in here for her too. She should find this cute, a little secret for her to discover, but her head and heart didn't agree.

She reached for the blue shape, but it was farther away than it seemed. She couldn't quite reach it. She stretched farther. She didn't remember crawling all the way into the little cupboard, but all of a sudden she was inside and it was dark.

When she was seven or eight, she had been playing in Poppa's basement, hunting through a large chest of his old clothes. She loved to play dress up with them, and one day she took all the clothes out and dumped them on the floor. She tied a bandana around her head and crawled inside, pretending it was a little boat and she was a pirate. When the top slammed shut, she had screamed and screamed.

She had only been stuck inside for a few minutes. Poppa came to the rescue, pulling her free from the chest, but dress up had been ruined forever. She would always remember that darkness within darkness, her own private pocket of hell.

She was there now. The musty smell and the velvety walls, too close to her limbs, unable to move or turn around. She reached forward quickly. Grab her purse and run, back out of here, but the object was not her purse at all. She didn't know what it was but it made her feel sick to touch it. It was a hat, an old fashioned hat, one of Nanny's and there must be a pin or something in it because it pricked her and drops of her blood squeezed out onto the floor. The wood sighed.

The dark closed in on her. She could hear breathing, too close. Gasping for air, she inched backwards. Time to get out of here. Her brain clanged in alarm. She couldn't breathe. She was suffocating. It was too dusty. Too dark. Her heels touched the wall. That wasn't right. That should be the door.

Jacalyn swung her head around but all was black. She couldn't see anything, not even her own hands in front of her. Tears leaked from her eyes. That breathing must be her. It had to be her. She reached out, but all she felt was walls, and where the fuck was the door where the fuck did the door go?

A low panicky sound escaped her lips. It didn't sound like her voice. It sounded like a small animal. She was out of her head and she opened her mouth to scream and something clenched around her waist, something dark and winding and scaled. Cloaked in darkness, it squeezed and she couldn't breathe and all she could do was scream and then Poppa was there.

His hands and arms were big, huge, encircling her like she was a child again. He swept her into his arms and pulled her out of the cupboard and held her in his lap. She pressed her face into the familiar scent of his warm flannel and hiccupped out sobs. He stroked her hair, her face, shushing her until she quieted and the sobs dissipated.

"Sweetheart, what were you doing in there?" She couldn't answer, just clung to him and cried. He pressed his cool hand against her clammy forehead. "My god, you're burning up!" He lifted her and she was weightless and she was flying, and in her tear-blurred vision, his face melted and shifted and writhed. So she closed her eyes.

CHAPTER 6

THE LIVING ROOM was small and cozy. Nanny and Poppa's wedding picture hung above the sofa. Jacalyn tried not to look at it. Their smiles were all wrong, too wide, sneering. Her head pulsed. She was sick, that was all.

Poppa settled her into his own comfy chair, nestled behind a table overflowing with books, calculators, remotes and gadgets. He wrapped a huge flannel blanket around her and brought her his own old man slippers. They flopped loose but comforting around her small feet.

He put the TV on while she waited. An old black and white movie. She couldn't pay attention to it, she was too busy concentrating on her breathing. The voices of the actors calmed her, even if she didn't quite understand them. The volume was too low. It didn't matter.

She could hear Poppa rattling around in the kitchen. She closed her eyes. She could picture him out there. He always made hot cocoa exactly the same way. It was a ritual. She had never been allowed to make it herself, had never wanted to. There was magic in the way he did it. He poured the milk in the smallest red pot, used only for cocoa and bought for cheap decades ago, back when things were built to last. He set the pot on the stove and heated the milk to scalding. While the milk was warming, he took three huge spoonfuls of the richest, deepest, darkest cocoa. That was something he never scaled back on, even when he was cutting corners everywhere else. Hot chocolate would not be economized. He put eight marshmallows in—*before* the hot milk, so they melted into a perfect gooey paste.

She could hear him humming to himself, shrill and off key. He came back into the living room at the exact moment she knew he would, with both mugs steaming and full.

He smiled at her. "Feeling a bit better? Well, this will fix you right up, all back to new." He pushed aside the debris on the table to set the cocoa in front of her. Scraps of paper floated to the floor. The writing on them was wrong, too black and thick and dark and mean to be her grandfather's.

"Thanks, Poppa." She was beginning to calm down again.

"Of course, sweetie. It's so good to have you here. So good to be able to take care of you again." He sat carefully on the sofa, stiff legs creaking, balancing his own mug of cocoa on the opposite side of the table. Without waiting for it to cool, he took a long swig, smacking his lips loudly in appreciation.

Jacalyn's mug was too hot to touch, left her skin red and sore. She would have to wait. She looked again for a clock.

"Poppa, what time is it? I hate to say it but . . . I have school in the morning. Work too. I really should . . . "

"Oh, you're hardly in the right state for that, darling. You need to rest. That's the only way to get better. You'll just have to miss a day or two."

"Oh." Did he expect her to stay here another night? Sick or not, she didn't even have any clothes here. God, what was wrong with her? Already dying to get away. She hadn't seen Poppa for almost six years. That last day. Something horrible had happened. Something she didn't want to think about. "Poppa, what . . . where have you been all this time?"

"I really don't want to talk about that, Jacalyn. Too many bad memories. I want us to start fresh. Do you really want to hash out those last few years again?"

Jacalyn's cheeks burned. She had been bad. She was only a teenager, but that was no excuse. She was never sure if he had known that she had taken the money—it hadn't been much, just a couple dollars here and there, but it had haunted her that she had never apologized. "Poppa, I'm so sorry."

His eyes wavered back and forth when he looked at her. "You could have just asked, you know. I would have given you money if I knew you needed it. I *did* give you money."

"I know, it was so stupid, I just . . . I was a teenager. I was showing off for my friends, I know that's not a good reason, but that's why."

"You were buying marijuana." He shook his head. "Such a disappointment to me. To me and your grandmother."

Tears sprang to her eyes. "Nanny knows, too?" Through the tears, through the confusion, she knew they were ignoring something more important. She raked trembling hands through her hair. "I took something else," she said, and that was closer to the truth and the thing lurking in the back of her brain took a step closer, pushed through the muddle.

"That's enough," Poppa said, his voice sharp. "I

don't want to talk about this shit, Jacalyn, I just want to enjoy an evening with you. Is that too much to ask?"

She lowered her eyes. Of course it wasn't. She shrank down in the chair. "I'm so sorry, Poppa."

He turned the television up. "Drink your hot chocolate."

It had cooled enough now. Her hands shook as she reached for the mug. She had barely eaten all day, but her stomach flipped unpleasantly at the scent of the chocolate. Something was wrong. Something was wrong. She drank deeply, and beneath the chocolate there were notes of bitter earth but she drank and she must have needed it because her thoughts felt smoother. Calmer.

She watched Poppa watch his show. The voices were loud but she still couldn't make out what they were saying. It was one of those old movies he liked to watch. It looked familiar, but she couldn't place it. The voices were speaking in English, but the words didn't seem to piece together right. She couldn't make sense of it. It was kind of funny.

She finished her hot chocolate. The taste it left in her mouth was unpleasant, but she felt better. Not as keyed up. Hot chocolate was a bedtime ritual, and it made her sleepy. She had slept all day. That was okay, she was sick. You were allowed to sleep when you were sick.

On the television, the actors seemed to have too many teeth. Too sharp. She blinked her eyes.

Poppa drank his hot chocolate. It looked different than hers, black and inky. It stuck to his lips and dribbled down his chin, making him look even older. The television howled.

BETTY ROCKSTEADY

She might have drifted off to sleep for a moment. When she woke, Poppa was in the middle of talking.

" . . . like that time those kids wanted to beat you up? Remember, Jacalyn? The little boys that lived across the street. They were younger than you, but you were so small back then. You didn't get your growth spurt 'til you were in your teens, so they were a lot bigger than you. Little bullies."

"I remember." Her throat felt thick.

"Rotten little brats. You were so shy. Awkward. Fat little thing you were, Nanny always thought your mom was feeding you too much. She was probably right. Anyway, they called you a fatty and said they were gonna beat you up, and you came crying to me. I fixed them for you, didn't I? Do you remember?"

"Yeah, of course I do, Poppa." She smiled. "You took off down the street and told them they better not mess with me, because you were a whole lot bigger than them. And they didn't after that. They left me alone."

Poppa nodded. "That's because I killed them."

Her eyes fluttered, breath left her nose and the blood drained from her face. "What did you say?"

"You heard me. They never bothered you again because I killed them. Little fuckers. I took that old baseball bat of your father's from the shed and I chased them down and bashed their little brains in." He chuckled.

Stars appeared in front of Jacalyn's eyes. The blanket around her tightened and she couldn't breathe. Had those boys disappeared? Her head spun. She couldn't remember if she had ever seen them again. "No . . . "

Her grandfather's laugh boomed, "Don't be so

naïve, Jacalyn! I'm just joking! Do you still believe everything anyone tells you? Just as gullible as you've always been." Poppa's smile was too wide and didn't fit his face. The blanket wound around her, too tight. She felt like she was going to pass out.

"Anyway." His cheerfulness sounded false. He leaped up, lighter on his feet than he had been in ages. "It's bedtime. You can finish watching this movie, but then off to bed. You need your rest, young lady."

The kiss he left on her forehead was dry as sand.

Jacalyn sat in front of the television for a while, not moving. The sounds from the TV were strange and looping. The movements of the actors were liquid, like they had no bones. They stared out of the screen at her, sweating and murmuring. They looked afraid. She clicked the television off and made her way to the door in the kitchen.

She rattled the doorknob as quietly as she could.

It was locked.

CHAPTER 7

SHE COULDN'T REMEMBER taking the slippers off, but the floor was sticky beneath her feet. Each footstep stuck to the ground, making a small sucking noise as she moved forward. The kitchen floor was filthy. Bachelorhood didn't agree with Poppa. She couldn't believe she hadn't noticed the stains earlier. It wasn't blood. It couldn't be blood. It must be that tomato juice from the fridge sticking to the soles of her feet. She stumbled toward the hallway.

The hallway dimensions distorted and the walls slanted at crazy angles. She swayed, balancing herself with a hand against the wall. It moved beneath her fingertips. She felt as though she were floating above herself. The hallway loomed ahead, long and dark and full of doors. Too many doors.

She brushed tears from her cheeks absentmindedly. She was just tired. She was sick. So she hadn't noticed some of the rooms; well, she had a lot on her mind. It was understandable. They couldn't have just appeared, they had to have been there all along. It was just a big apartment. A really big apartment.

She opened the door nearest the kitchen. It should have been the room she slept in, she was sure it was, but instead it was another bathroom. Sort of. The room was tiny with sickly green walls. The only furniture it contained was an old fashioned tub and a crooked mirror, hanging on the wall across from her. Jacalyn was alarmed at how sallow her face looked.

She didn't look in the tub. She wouldn't look in the tub.

She closed the door and felt better instantly. She didn't like the rooms here. Something was wrong with them.

Why the fuck was Poppa living here on his own? Why wasn't he at home, where he belonged?

The next door wasn't her room either. It was the bad door again. Heat thrummed through the doorknob and she yanked her hand back. It was too late, the door creaked open. She shouldn't have looked. It didn't make sense. Apartments didn't have basements, but the stairs cascaded down and the wooden steps did not look safe and he should have checked them. He should have replaced them. He had replaced everything else in the goddamn house. She shut that door too.

Her room was the next door and the rush of relief at seeing those yellow walls was quickly tempered with a sickening feeling as her stomach dropped.

Something had happened.

It was a mess. Books and ornaments were knocked around haphazardly, spilling off the shelves. Broken green glass sprawled across the floor like a trap. Most of the books had been torn apart.

The tears were coming again. She recognized her childhood nursery rhyme book amongst the wreckage. It had taken a lot of damage, cardboard covers ripped and torn, the remaining pages singed and mangled. Scraps of paper had been ripped out and spread across the floor, cruel writing scrawled across them. Picking her way carefully across the glass, Jacalyn scooped up a few pages.

All the pages weren't from the nursery rhyme books. Mixed in were pages torn from another book. Not *her* witchcraft book, the one she had lent Poppa to read, but a stranger one. A worse one. The symbols on the pages were dizzying, made her stomach feel wormy. The bright pretty pictures from the nursery rhyme books had been changed. The smiling faces had their eyes torn out. She couldn't make out all the words that had been written on the pages, but the ones she could read were horrible.

LIAR

THIEF

The witchcraft book she had lent to Poppa lay across the bed, ripped in half, smeared with . . . something. It smelled bad. The book was several inches thick but had been ripped through in one clean motion. Poppa wouldn't be strong enough to do that. Would he?

Across the cover, in the same writing: BITCH.

Is that really what he thought of her? Jacalyn felt miserable. Tears came hot and quick. She would never sleep after this. He had been kind to her so far, and she had felt like he wanted her here, but this was awful. Had he gone crazy? She had apologized but it wasn't enough.

She *was* guilty, wasn't she? Something started to creep into her thoughts, begging her to look at it, but she pushed it away. She was afraid to think about it. She wouldn't think about it.

But she had stolen from him. She had ignored him. She had been an ungrateful little brat. He had been angry at her and he lashed out and tore this room apart and it made her feel sick and sad deep in her stomach. This was her fault. Her actions had consequences, and she had ruined her relationship with her Poppa. A hard knot formed between her eyebrows.

She was awful. She had always known she was awful.

She sat on the bed with her torn book in her hands. She was pathetic. She had to stop feeling sorry for herself. This was her fault and she had to face up to it. She deserved his anger. She had obviously hurt him very much, and even now that she was here, she wasn't acting how she should. She should have been thrilled to see him but all she had done was sleep and complain that she wanted to go home.

Oh god, Mom must be so worried. And Nanny. She cried harder. She was doing the exact same thing again, wasn't she? Slacking off and zoning out and being unappreciative of her family.

She got to her feet again. What was she supposed to do now? She couldn't keep making the same bad choices. Nanny had been so sick last week, but she had just gone out drinking like it didn't even matter. These were the times she should be spending with her, but she was still putting herself first. Hadn't she learned? She needed to get a hold of them now, the stress of this was the last thing Mom and Nanny needed. God, what was wrong with her? She thought just because she was older and had a job and finished high school that she was doing so much better, but she was still the same shitty person she had always been.

Okay. She had to do something about that, but

first she had to talk to Poppa. Apologize. Make him understand she had changed. Or at least that she wanted to change. And then maybe they could talk about getting her home.

CHAPTER 8

MAYBE SHE SHOULD have just lay down. The hallway writhed. Sweat soaked her back. She couldn't stand to ignore this any longer, it only got worse the longer she avoided it. Once she talked to Poppa and got everything settled with him, then she would sleep.

She planted a hand against the wall to steady herself. Her vision doubled. There were too many doors. "Poppa?" Something murmured, something else rustled. Everything was so dark. She should have stayed in her room.

Down the hallway, she could hear voices. Chanting. He must be listening to the radio before bed. She had always found that sound comforting, soft voices that rose and fell as she drifted off to sleep. They didn't sound so comforting tonight. They sounded angry. Static whined and crackled as she approached the door. She listened. He must be awake still, there was no snoring. He either didn't hear her or he was ignoring her.

She shifted her weight, indecisive. Would it be better to wait until morning? No. She couldn't keep putting things off. She had to talk to him now. "Poppa," she called again, and rapped her knuckles gently against the door.

A barking cough as he cleared his throat. He hacked and rolled phlegm in his mouth. There was a sickening splat as spit hit the floor. She drew her hand back.

"Door's open, come on in, sweetheart."

Jacalyn gagged on the fecal smell as she opened the door. The room was tiny and filthy, barely big enough for Poppa's bed and radio. Poppa lay stretched out on the bed, naked but for a dirty pair of briefs. His chest was sunken in, limbs emaciated. His thighs were covered with disgusting wounds and rotted flesh. She choked, eyes watering. God, what was that smell?

Poppa sat up, his flaccid penis bouncing beneath the thin underwear. "Come on, sit down." He patted the grey sheet next to him. There was a knife on it, a smear of blood staining the sheet.

She recoiled, stomach shifting uncomfortably. "Um, I'm sorry, I didn't . . . I don't want to disturb you, Poppa."

"Nonsense. You wanted something, didn't you?" A hard gleam lit his eyes. "I said, sit down."

The bed was low to the ground and she shuffled on to it. She folded her hands in her lap, not wanting to touch the grimy material beneath her. His thin arm brushed against hers, making her skin crawl. She kept her eyes on the thin sliver of the hallway she could see. She wanted to keep her gaze as far away from the filthy bulge in Poppa's pants as she could. It was so hard to sit up straight. Even the brief walk from her room had made her dizzy.

"You don't look well, Jacalyn. Can I get you something? Is that why you came to see me, because you need something?"

LIKE JAGGED TEETH

She wiped her clammy hands against the nightdress. "No. I'm okay. I'm fine. I just wanted . . . I saw what you did in my room. I saw . . . " She looked up at him. She wanted to apologize but the words caught in her throat. Something was wrong with Poppa. His eyes went too deep and when she looked into them, the whole room pulsed around her. A cockroach scurried from beneath the bed, brushing against her feet, making her scream.

"What is it, baby-doll? What is it?" His voice came from nowhere. His mouth never opened. The radio screamed out blasts of static. The darkness in his eyes revealed sharp teeth that gnashed and spat. His skin flaked away to reveal thick ropes of meat. The smell of rot accompanied the thick black smoke that unwound from him, choking her again.

Jacalyn fell to the floor, coughing. She needed to run but she couldn't move, could barely get enough air. Tears streamed down her cheeks and she coughed and the room expanded around her, and she couldn't crawl out the door because it was miles away. She coughed and coughed and her mouth filled with something thick and meaty and awful. She spat it out, and through her tears saw a vicious slug that writhed on the floor, hissing at her. Then Poppa's hands were beneath her armpits. He lifted her up and she looked into his eyes and it was him again, and she felt so weak and confused.

"You're sick." His voice was slow and warped, a record played backwards. "What are you doing running around like this when you're so sick? You should be in your bed."

"I wanted to apologize to you." The words were hard to get out. It was hard enough just to breathe.

His eyes were cold and dark. "You're sick, baby-doll. Go back to your room. I don't like it when you disobey me."

"I'm sorry, Poppa." The room spun. Poppa's eyes bulged and dripped down his cheeks. The walls peeled, revealing rotten wood beneath. She needed to lie down. She lurched from the room, sweating, feeling worse with each moment that passed. He didn't get up to help her. He didn't forgive her. How could he? She didn't even know how to apologize.

Shadowy figures accompanied her back to her room. She stumbled through the door. The strange messy room was a comfort compared to that awful hallway. None of it was real. She was sick. She was so sick. She had never been sick enough to see things like that before.

Glass crunched beneath her bare foot and she moaned.

She hopped to the side of the room and placed her hand against the swirling wallpaper. She breathed in deep before she looked.

A huge chunk of green glass jabbed out of her heel, dripping blood onto the floor.

"Oh shit, oh shit." Just looking at the misshapen piece of glass protruding from her flesh made her wobble. The blood rushed from her head.

She hobbled to the door. Pain shot through her foot into her calf. She had to get to the bathroom and get this out. Clean it somehow in that filthy tub.

As soon as she placed her hand on the doorknob, something shifted outside the door. Something huge.

"Poppa . . . " Was he standing out there, waiting? Checking on her, or waiting for a real apology?

But the groan was too deep, too loud. Her hand floated away from the doorknob.

LIKE JAGGED TEETH

Something wasn't right.

Her foot throbbed and the panic that swirled around her head was not to be ignored. The noises from the hall were wet and wrong and slobbering and she could not leave the room. She would not.

She backed up, made her way to the bed.

She couldn't take any more. She needed to rest. Nothing made sense and everything hurt.

Her brain went blank. She was floating. She sat on the bed, shaking. The room was hot and she was exhausted. The pain in her foot was dull and distant and she wanted to ignore it, but every time she moved, the glass brushed against the sheets and she couldn't stand it. She yanked the glass out of her foot, splashing her hands with gore.

Her eyes were so heavy.

She slept. Blood spread across the bedsheets and eventually the sounds in the hallway stopped.

CHAPTER 9

THE BED WAS too soft, then too hard. Her foot hurt, but the pain was far away. She opened her eyes and waited for the shadows to come into focus, but there was only swirling darkness.

The walls were too close. She was suffocating.

Raspy breath closed in on her. Her own came hot and quick. Theirs came slithering nearer, cold and foreign. The sour scent of sweat and booze made her dizzy.

Nothing felt right.

Her chest was so tight it ached. The darkness was oppressive and maddening. She blinked over and over. She was blind. But if you were blind, it wasn't really dark, was it? It was nothing. And this darkness felt like something. A thick wet blanket that surrounded her. She crept backwards until her back hit the wall. It expanded and contracted against her, soft and pliant as flesh. Her breath came faster, shallow, panicked. The darkness enveloped. The darkness took everything else away. She wanted to reach out for the lamp but she was afraid that her hands would creep away and what they felt would not be the comforting surface of the lamp, they would creep over flesh and bone and blood and she would start screaming and she would never be able to stop.

She wanted to call to Poppa. She wanted him to swoop in and rescue her but she was afraid. She was a child again, afraid in the night and she needed her Poppa, but her voice was dead in her throat and did she even deserve to have him save her?

Her foot ached and she drew it closer to her body but she could not see it. Each movement shot fresh hot pain through her calf, working its way up into her thigh. Her cheeks were wet and she sat so still, not making a sound but for her breathing.

There was something in the room with her. Large and slithering and wrong. All the things she once thought lived under the bed and in closets were here, in this room, and Poppa too, Poppa was one of the things now. He was naked and bleeding and his eyes were full of teeth and nothing would ever be okay again. She couldn't call to him because he was there already.

She couldn't see him but she could feel him.

Creeping across the floor, dragging himself by broken fingernails towards her bed, where she sat small and defenseless in the dark.

Time passed in a vacuum. She couldn't tell if it was moments later or hours when the sun crept up, changing the darkness in gradual increments to vicious red shadows. Moment by moment the room was revealed to be just the same as she had left it last night, strewn with glass and paper and chaos, but safe.

Her foot throbbed. She was afraid to look at it. She was afraid to know, as though the pain would become clearer when she saw the devastation of her injury.

BETTY ROCKSTEADY

The room was bathed in light. Her head swam. Something was very, very wrong. No wonder she felt so awful and afraid and everything was so strange. She was sick. She had a fever. And she had lost a lot of blood.

The sheet was dark and sticky and pasted to her foot. She tried to pry it away but just choked on her pain. The bedding was thick with blood, mushy and red. She needed to see the damage, but she was afraid to touch it. Her heart beat in her chest, a small panicked bird. She pulled on the sheet and screamed again. She wanted Poppa, but she was afraid to call to him. She wanted her mother, but Mom didn't even know where she was.

She could just leave the sheet on, a makeshift bandage, but everything in the room was so filthy and the thought of that dirt leaking into her wound sent a rush of panic through her and she peeled it away, quick, just like a band aid and it tore and she screamed and screamed and her head went light and faint and Poppa didn't come.

She heard him in the kitchen, humming to himself.

Her foot was huge and throbbing. The wound was ragged across her heel and dribbled rivulets of dark blood. Too much blood. Deep purple bruising and threads of darkness ran up her calf. Oh god. It was infected, that's why everything felt so strange. She needed to go to the doctor.

"Poppa," she croaked. And again, louder, "Poppa, I need a doctor. I hurt myself."

He didn't answer but she could hear him in the kitchen. A sickly sweet smell of oatmeal wafted into the room, intermingled with the earthen scent of blood and decay.

LIKE JAGGED TEETH

Jacalyn stood up and light flickered across her vision. She almost fell back, but she didn't let herself. She couldn't. She didn't want to pass out again. She needed to get out of here, for sure now. She needed a doctor.

She slumped against the wall and staggered across the room, careful not to step on any more of that awful glass. The walls wavered. It took a long time to get across the room. It contracted and expanded, like the room itself were breathing.

A trail of blood and pus extended behind her. She pushed her way through the door. She was sick and sticky, she could smell the sweat that soaked her nightgown. The door was heavy but she pushed and stumbled, not into the hall but directly into the kitchen and Poppa was there and he smiled at her and something wasn't right.

CHAPTER 10

"**J**ACALYN, I THOUGHT you were going to miss breakfast." Poppa's smile had too many teeth. His face stretched, wrinkles upon wrinkles spider webbing across his cheeks. Were his eyes always so dark?

Jacalyn leaned against the fridge, dripping with sweat. "I need a doctor, my foot . . . " She glanced down and the blood trickling from her wound made her feel even weaker. "I hurt my foot." Her voice sounded like it was coming from miles away.

"Tsk, tsk, you can be awful clumsy." Poppa smiled again. "Have a seat, we'll get that fixed up."

"I don't think . . . " but it was too much work to talk. It was too much work to walk. She slipped in the blood as she moved forward, cracking her chin against the floor. She groaned. "Poppa, I'm sick. Please. Can you take me to the doctor? I need help." Her vision blurred. Poppa's face narrowed. He looked like a vulture, beak sharp and vicious, ready to tear her apart. These thoughts were not her own. The floor was cool against her hot skin.

"I want to have breakfast first. Get up, you little shit, and eat the breakfast I made."

Her confusion began to break and she felt the first

real trickle of fear snaking in. There was no time to think. No time to get a grip on things. Poppa's hands reached beneath her, lifting her up too easily, like a baby. In one swift motion, he planted her in the kitchen chair. Her foot smacked against the table and she groaned, lowering her head. A shaky breath and a moment passed before Poppa slammed a bowl down in front of her.

"Jacalyn, eat your fucking porridge."

She blinked her eyes open and stared into the sludgy paste. It was thick and gluey, and a drop of yellowish fluid swirled within. Nausea burbled up her throat and she gagged. Through watery eyes, she looked across the table where Poppa sat. He ate ravenously. The gruel smeared across his chin and dribbled down his shirt. The taste of bile filled Jacalyn's mouth.

"Eat up! I didn't make this breakfast for you to stare at it."

Tears spilled from Jacalyn's eyes. She was hot and sick and confused and she didn't like being yelled at. "Poppa, please, my foot hurts so bad. I think something's wrong."

"*You think something's wrong,*" he imitated, his voice a song. He pounded his fist against the table, spilling salt into the mess he had made beneath his bowl. "Your little foot hurts and you turn into a fucking crybaby. I've had a whole lot worse happen to me, and you don't see me complaining!" His voice was shrill. "Do you remember what happened to me, Jacalyn? When you hurt your fucking foot, do you remember what happened to me?"

Jacalyn sobbed. Pain pounded deep inside her brain and it hurt and screamed and she was so, so scared now and something was coming. She could feel it rearing back, ready to pounce and she cried, "I want my mom, please, please."

Poppa leaped from the table. Too fast. Too agile. "Fine. Let's get this over with."

Jacalyn was boneless. She was weightless. Poppa yanked her back to her feet painfully. He slung her arm over his shoulder and dragged her to the hallway.

"Where's the phone? I thought the phone was in the kitchen."

In the hallway there was just one door. Trickles of panic built into a crescendo. The hallway swam around her and her ears filled with a maddening static. "No, no,"

Poppa twisted the doorknob and it was the bad door and she didn't want to go down there, she didn't want to see it.

"Poppa, no, I wanna call my mom the phone's not there let me go let me go." She didn't know she still had strength in her but as the door creaked open she scrabbled against Poppa and she hit him and he was too strong and he opened the door and the stairs gaped up at her, broken like wooden teeth and Poppa threw her and she fell down, down, down the stairs into the basement.

CHAPTER 11

THE STEPS SMACKED against her back and her neck. Her hands flew up to protect her face, automatic. She curled into herself, covering her eyes. She wouldn't look. She wouldn't look. Her foot banged against a stair and she groaned but kept her eyes shut tight. Her hands and feet scrambled for purchase but it was no good. She could feel the bruises forming already, she knew exactly how they would look, purple and brown and taking weeks to fade, each one a reminder of her guilt. She deserved the ugliness.

The last stairs crumbled under her weight and she kept her eyes shut so tight. She landed on something soft and mushy and too warm and she screamed and scrabbled away from it into the stench of rotten fruit. Her hands and feet and knees were full of glass and her nightgown was soaked through and it wasn't water, it was wine and blood and it wasn't okay and it would never be okay again.

She ignored the pain and she tried to pull herself away but the thing was moving and it couldn't be moving, it should be dead.

A cold hand grabbed her ankle and she howled.

"Jacalyn," Poppa moaned, "Jacalyn, what are you doing down here?"

"No." She kicked him away and crawled across the broken glass and it couldn't be him it wasn't him because he's dead and suddenly her mind was clear and she doesn't want to remember but she does.

Oh god, she does.

CHAPTER 12

SHE STOPPED BY in the afternoon to sneak down the basement and leave the window open. He had so much homemade wine, he'd never notice a couple of bottles missing. She told Tanya and Damon she could get booze for sure, and maybe she had been overconfident but it would be fun. It would be worth it. But now that the moment had come, she was more scared than she thought she'd be. Taking a few bucks here and there hadn't been a big deal. Poppa left change all over the place and he never noticed it missing. But taking a few bottles of wine; that was a little trickier. That took some finesse.

She waited 'til after 10:00. Nanny and Poppa would be in bed and she would be quiet enough that they would never know the difference. It seemed like a great plan when she came up with it, but now that she was actually sneaking around in the dark, it was a whole different ball game. She felt guilty and sneaky and her heart was pounding a thousand beats a minute because what if she got caught? How would she explain?

Simple. She just wouldn't get caught.

So before she met up with her friends she just walked by Poppa's house. The streets were empty. It would be a cinch. She casually walked through his yard and slid the window aside and fuck, her boots were big and black and heavy and they would be too loud. She took a second to untie the laces and stash them in a bush and she slid down and oh shit she already fucked it up. She landed too hard, the boxes stacked beneath her fell and the noise they made was too loud and oh fuck, what was she going to do now?

Okay, fine, adrenaline rushing heart beating brow sweating, it's okay, its already too late, so grab the booze and get out of here, it would just look like a break in and she could deal with it later and

"Who's there?"

Fuck.

"I hear you down there, we're calling the police!"

Her hands were sweaty around the bottles and could she even get out the window now? What if Nanny was watching out the window, oh god, she had fucked this all up.

"Get back here," she heard Nanny hiss, "Don't go down there, shut the door, let the police take care of it."

Yes, please, please let the police take care of it, Poppa, don't come down here, oh fuck what am I going to do?

But Poppa was not that kind of man. He had fought in wars. He had been an intimidating figure once and his feet slammed on the step but he was not a big man anymore, he was old and his heart was weak and she heard the sound he made and it was an awful sound, a guttural sound and she saw his silhouette in the light at the top of the stairs and he clutched his chest—

And oh god, he fell.

LIKE JAGGED TEETH

The stairs broke and crumbled and snapped beneath his weight. He reached out uselessly and grasped at the banister but he was tumbling and Nanny was screaming and Jacalyn was screaming and he let out one more pained sound and she heard the exact moment when his neck snapped and he sprawled out before her and the bottles dropped from her sweaty hands and they broke and—

His head wasn't on right. A bone jutted out from his leg. He was shattered and he was broken and his eyes bulged and they stared into her.

She fell to her knees in the broken glass and she reached for him and the shards of broken wine bottles stuck in her hands and feet and she hurt her foot so bad and his eyes looked into hers and asked

What have you done what have you done what have you done

CHAPTER 13

POPPA REACHED FOR HER. His eyes were milk-white, rolling blind in their sockets. His head dangled from his crumpled neck. He groaned, and the sharp taste of bile rose in the back of her throat. The air was damp with the scent of cheap homemade wine.

"Jacalyn . . . please, help me . . . "

Everything in her body screamed to run. This couldn't be real. None of this could be real. But there he was in front of her, crying and bleeding and god, what had she done? How had she let this happen?

"Poppa." She pulled herself forward with blood-stained hands.

"Jacalyn? Is that you? Honey, I can't see you. Come closer," he wheezed.

Guilt was a swamp inside her gut. She had done this. It was her fault. "Poppa, I'm so sorry," she wept. She took his hand and his eyes rolled up to her.

"You did this." His voice was thick with phlegm. His hand was freezing in hers, yanking her closer.

"I'm sorry, I'm sorry, I'm sorry." She couldn't stop. This was all out of control. She was cold and damp and she was shivering, wet with blood and wine and tears and how could she have made such a mistake? How had she *forgotten*? She had thought of it every day of her whole fucking life and she had just *forgotten*.

"I'm dying and it's your fault," he croaked. "You killed me and I don't care what your fucking therapist says, it's your fault and I blame you."

Tears came thick and hot but they cleared her head.

"Nanny blames you."

It wasn't true. It wasn't.

"Everyone blames you."

He looked at her and his eyes went black.

The urge to hold him and comfort him as he died shrank back into a small cold thing in her brain. His wrinkled skin rippled. Bone protruded, broken and jagged. Shapes bulged and tented beneath his skin. A thread of truth wormed through her brain. Despite what her eyes told her, this was not Poppa and that fucking thing upstairs was not Poppa. Poppa was dead and the walls closed in tighter.

Her eyes were wide and his were dead and his teeth looked too sharp. She started to back away. His hand snaked out, too quick for such an old man, wrapped tight and painful around her bare ankle. His grip was cold, too cold, it froze her to the bone and he squeezed and Jacalyn screamed.

He pulled her down, closer to him. His mouth opened wide, rows of sharp teeth glistened wet in the grey light.

"Baby-doll, you're so sweet," he rasped. A long, wet tongue slithered out of his mouth. The noises that came out of her didn't sound like her own. His tongue caressed the wound on her foot, sandpaper rough. The pain was hotter than fire and she couldn't stop screaming and screaming and her hands flailed and she grabbed a wine bottle and swung and it smashed. When the glass embedded in his face he just laughed, but he let go. He let go and she fell, crashed into the boxes all over again, and she heard a pattering of feet from upstairs. The door opened.

"Who's there?" Poppa called and he stood at the top of the stairs and she *couldn't stop screaming* and her voice was hoarse and ragged and the thing in the basement with her, the nasty rotten broken thing started to stand up.

A breeze from the open window rustled Jacalyn's hair and the creature the thing that wasn't Poppa couldn't be Poppa stood up on broken bones and it creaked and stretched and everything about it was wrong.

But it was slow.

And upstairs, Poppa tumbled down the first step and he made a sound, it was an awful sound and Jacalyn pushed the trunk she had once been trapped inside beneath the window and hauled herself out, ignoring the screaming pain in her foot. She felt its breath hot behind her but she scrabbled and climbed and pulled herself out the window and there was no fresh air, there was no way outside and there was no relief.

CHAPTER 14

SHE WAS IN the kitchen. Her breathing was frantic and thin and she was not okay. She tumbled through the door and her hands were on the doorknob instantly, twisting and shaking. The door was locked and it wouldn't open and she spun the knob and put her shoulder into it and screamed but it didn't budge.

"How could you forget what you did to me?"

Jacalyn pressed her forehead against the door and closed her eyes. She hadn't forgotten. She had never forgotten, not for one single day, what she had done. What was happening here wasn't right. It wasn't natural.

"It's okay, baby-doll. We have all the time in the world to make up for it now. Over and over again. You forget, I remind you. That's the plan." Dry fingers brushed her shoulder and she spun around, blinked back tears.

Poppa grinned at her—not Poppa, it didn't even look like Poppa anymore. It was a hideous caricature of who Poppa had been. His wrinkles were sinister, not outlined in kindness. His smile twisted, blurred. The bones beneath his flesh didn't connect how they should. There were too many joints, everything long and angular. His eyes were dark as universes, spinning madly in their sockets. She couldn't breathe.

He sat at the table, peering at her around a bottle of wine. She didn't want to look at the plates. She didn't know what was on them, but it was wet and red and meaty.

"Sit with me, sweetheart." His voice echoed in the small kitchen. Jacalyn's knees shook. Her throat was too dry to answer, she made a low croaking sound. This wasn't happening. This couldn't be happening. Oh god, why did she have to remember?

"Jacalyn, sit the fuck down with your Poppa and eat your breakfast." He pounded his huge fist against the table, making it tremble. "Or do you just want to disappoint me again?"

"You're not my Poppa." She hated the way her voice shook, but she spat out the truth. This was not her Poppa and she was trapped and she was so afraid.

"What the fuck did you say?" He was on his feet. He darted forward. His hand crunched around her wrist, making her gasp as he yanked her to the table. He held so tightly, her delicate wrist bones ached. She let herself be led, not knowing what else to do. His grip was strong and she was small and weak.

He shoved her into the chair. It wobbled beneath her, but he steadied it. He grasped her shoulders with rough hands and looked at her face and for a moment he looked like Poppa again, but it was a thin curtain of a lie. She could see it in his eyes, there was no escape and the fear licked its way up her throat and if she started screaming she would never stop and what the fuck *was* this thing.

"I'm your Poppa and you better remember that, you little bitch." The inside of his mouth was wet and red and she sat as still as she could, unable to open her mouth to reply. "Now you stay in your seat there or I'll make you fucking regret it. We're going to have a nice breakfast together. Just Poppa and his special girl." It let go of her and she smelled sulfur and where it had touched her, she was numb and strange and so she sat, too terrified to budge.

The Poppa thing sat across from her, movements quick and liquid. She didn't move. She couldn't.

He stared at her while he lifted the plate up to his snout. His vicious tongue slithered out, black and scaled. It rasped down his chin and lapped up the gore. He slurped and chewed. Something red leaked out, misting his face and the table. He narrowed his eyes to slits, eyebrows knotting together. "Eat your breakfast, Jacalyn." There was a warning tone in his voice and a hunk of meat dropped out of his mouth when he spoke.

The thing on her plate was throbbing, meaty and discolored, a diseased organ. There wasn't enough air in here. She couldn't think. Her feet dangled from the chair, inches from the ground. She wanted to get down. She wanted to curl up and sleep. She was crying again, she couldn't stop. She was going to throw up. "I don't feel good. Please, I don't feel good."

"You're never going to get your strength up if you don't eat." Shadows pulsed behind him. He was miles away. "Be a good little girl." He smiled, broken wooden stairs for teeth. "We can stay here all night if we have to."

Her stomach cramped. "No . . . I'm not hungry . . . " She couldn't stop crying. "Please, I want my mommy. I want to see my mommy." Her head hurt so bad, she couldn't think. Looking at him made her dizzy, made her sick. She wanted to get back in her room. The room that was supposed to be her room. She needed to think. She couldn't think with its eyes on her. She didn't want to eat this food, nothing felt right when she ate his food.

His eyes were sharks, savage with teeth. "You've got to eat. Get your strength up. You've been so sick. Just try a little bit. You've always been a picky eater, but sometimes when you try things you like them."

She broke his gaze. She hated to do it. Shadows flickered in her peripherals and it felt so very dangerous not to keep an eye on him. But he gestured and she looked at her plate and gagged. Meat and bone glared back up at her and she felt the bile coming up. "I can't . . . " Something in the meat looked familiar, a section of freckled cheek, a piece of a smile. Her head bobbed on her neck, sank to her chest. *If I faint I'll land face-first in this shit.*

"Fine. At least drink your wine." He smashed the top of the bottle against the table, breaking it open. The sudden sound made her scream. Her nerves were too tightly wound and the scent of the homemade wine was too sharp and too awful and the feeling of panic would not be abated, it seemed impossible, but it kept getting worse and it was too much and she choked back a giggle. She was insane and he was coming closer.

"No—" she said, but he moved so quick, he was right next to her, slamming the wine bottle down, nearly banging it against her hand.

"What do you mean, no? You disobedient little shit. After all I've done for you! After all you've done to me." The Poppa thing was too big for the kitchen. It pulled itself up to its full height, slouching beneath the ceiling. Its shoulders angled out like antlers. The shape of its skull protruded beneath thin skin. Every time it opened its mouth she could see the teeth, too many teeth and it kept talking and she didn't want to hear its perverted voice, it wasn't Poppa it wasn't Poppa it wasn't Poppa. "I thought this was so fucking important to you, so important you would kill for it. You wanted this wine, now fucking drink it."

His hand was huge and strong and clamped against the back of her head. Jacalyn tried to pull away. She kicked her legs and the chair shook but the Poppa thing pulled her to her feet by her hair and she opened her mouth to scream again and he poured the wine down her throat. Shards of glass nicked her cheeks and tongue. Fresh blood swirled into rotten fruit. The bittersweet flavor stung her mouth, hurt worse than the glass as it wormed into her esophagus. Her gut responded with bile, shooting up past her tongue and dribbling down her chin. "Do you like that, baby-doll? Is that what you wanted?" He laughed and he kept pouring and she couldn't breathe and she spat wine into his face and he dropped her.

The back of her head slammed against the tile and she curled up on the floor and she couldn't take this anymore. Everything tasted like blood.

"You little bitch." He wiped the spit from his face. "You listen to your Poppa or you're going to regret it."

"You're not my Poppa," she screamed, finally the words came and she was so angry and she couldn't stop, "My Poppa is dead and I don't know what you are, but you're not him! You're not my Poppa!"

The thing snarled. Its eyes were black holes and the room closed in and he grabbed her hair again, yanking a handful out. She kicked her legs against the floor and he hauled her out into the hall and oh god if she went down into the basement again she would die, she couldn't do this again, she would rather let it eat her.

"I want to go home. I want to go home I want to go home I want to go home."

He ripped the door open. "You're not going anywhere. You're staying here as long as I want you. You're fucking grounded." He shoved her forward, and it was her room and she was bleeding and her skin was raw but she was so relieved to see those yellow walls. "Let me know when you're ready to apologize." The door slammed shut and she almost felt like she could breathe.

CHAPTER 15

SHAKY LEGS, SHAKY ARMS, the room spun and she let herself collapse, pressed her back against the door. She could hear it out there, still talking to itself. She couldn't understand what it was saying. The words were guttural and strange. The room was spinning and her foot hurt so fucking much and none of this made sense.

Poppa would never do this to her. Poppa wouldn't want her to suffer but her guts twisted with knives and she deserved it, didn't she? Whatever this was, it was her fault.

The wallpaper writhed and she shut her eyes tight. Her mouth tasted like that shitty wine and blood and she wished she had more, she wished she was so drunk she couldn't think because none of this made any fucking sense and her throat hurt from screaming and she needed something, god.

Jacalyn curled tighter on the floor. Tears leaked from tightly shut lids. Everything here was strange and awful and she didn't want to look at it anymore. Her head felt thick and pained, her throat ached from screaming. She wiped her eyes, dry and chapped from tears.

She wanted to sleep but she was too cold. She wanted anything but to be here.

BETTY ROCKSTEADY

She stayed still and nothing changed. She just grew colder and more awake but eventually the awful shuffling sounds quieted. She was alone in the darkness behind her eyes and had hours passed, or only minutes?

She wanted to go home.

She smelled cigarette smoke. Familiar, unwanted. Bad habits die hard, because it woke a craving somewhere deep inside her. She hadn't smoked in years, not since Nanny had first gotten sick, but now the need opened like a mouth inside her. Something, anything, to distract. To take away all this pain.

Her eyes were chapped from crying and it hurt to open them. Smoke lingered in the air, wet and grey and damp, obscuring the corners of the room.

She was cold. Her foot ached and bled. It would never stop bleeding. She would die here, pale and tired on the hard floor. Her bones groaned in protest as she pulled herself back to her feet. She wanted a blanket. She wanted to die. She wanted to escape. There had to be a way.

The floor was still strewn with paper and glass. It wasn't safe. She grabbed a book that was mostly unscathed and used it to sweep aside the debris. Papers swirled through the air lazily, as if caught on a breeze, although the air was thick and stagnant.

Her foot throbbed. She needed to bandage it. She stumbled toward the bed. The sheets were filthy, worse than they had been last night. Tiny bugs with razor teeth ate away at them. Her head pounded. She slouched on the bed with her head between her knees, then finally ripped a strip off the bottom of her nightgown. The thin material tore easily. She wrapped it clumsily around her foot. The blood slowed but didn't stop. She fingered the sheet beneath her. Ripping the bandage had given her an idea.

She crawled across the bed to the window. Even before she pressed her face against it, she knew the drop would be too far. She would never make it. But she had to try *something*. She couldn't stay here. She couldn't face that thing again. The glass was icy cold against her hands. The latch on the window was rusted shut. She pressed her hand against it but it wouldn't budge. Anger reared up, shocking in its intensity, a scream burbled in her throat but she kept it in, even as she slammed her hand, again and again against the latch. She would fucking break it if she had to, but she wouldn't stay here any longer. She wouldn't. She couldn't.

With one last thrust, the hard metal of the latch sliced her flesh and blood sprayed out of the palm of her hand. She shrieked and heard a deep, throaty giggle from somewhere in the room. Jacalyn spun, her eyes darting to the corners and back again. They were dark, bathed in clouds of dust and smoke. The other side of the room was miles away now. She turned away, back to the window and miracle of miracles, as though the blood had loosened it, the latch finally turned and she slid the window open.

The fresh air crashed against her face and she gulped it in. God, she felt almost human again. The air in this apartment was poison and her head felt clearer than it had in days. She stuck her head out.

There was no one outside to hear her screams.

The ground was too far away. Way too far away. The sick feeling in her stomach spread and the tears were coming and she was sick of being so weak. She was sick of feeling guilty.

BETTY ROCKSTEADY

There was something out there. She couldn't see it, but she could feel it. In the distance, buildings shifted. The moon was full and fat and ripe. The stars were all wrong.

There was nothing for her outside and there was nothing for her here.

Something flew by the window, shrieking, and Jacalyn fell back into the room, cracking her back against the floor. Her head sank. Her mind felt dull.

It was too much. She couldn't take anything else in. Nothing made sense and everything was wretched. She would just lay here, forever, not moving, until she died. Because that was what this was about, wasn't it? She had done wrong, she had wronged her poor Poppa and now she had to pay, and she would. She just wished it would be over already.

The ceiling sank closer. Black mold rorschached across faded yellow stains; filthy, like everything else in this fucking place. She could make out shapes in the curls of flaking paint. Everything hurt so she didn't move. She was heavy. Immobile. The paint peeled, flaked, drifted down to her. It hit her skin and sizzled, leaving oily smears where it touched. She didn't care.

The walls closed in, inch by inch.

Wallpaper peeled away, revealed shadowy figures, indecipherable drawings.

She waited.

In the hallway, it moved. It sang that fucking lullaby and it wasn't Poppa and Poppa would never want this for her. She felt fingers brush through her hair and in a flash she saw Poppa, the real Poppa and she got up so fast she nearly fell over. She bit her lip and pushed past the dizziness and whatever was outside the window had to be better than what was in here.

The air was cold and the ground was miles away.

She would never survive the fall, but if she used the sheets on the bed. And the blankets. There were a few of them, and she could tie them to the bedpost and maybe, maybe it would get her close enough that she could drop to the ground and only break a few bones. Or maybe someone else in the apartment below would see her and help her, as if this was a normal building. As if there was an escape. She choked the tears back down. She had to try. Poppa would want her to try.

She pushed her doubts aside. If she stopped now she would collapse into a puddle of fear and pain and her head would cloud and who knew what it would take to shock her out of it this time. The room was expanding outward and the air was too stuffy to breathe, the scent of smoke was so thick. She coughed the cough of a long-time smoker. She coughed like Nanny.

She threw her head back out the window and gulped in air. The room was too warm. The air was thick and she couldn't breathe and she took a last deep breath to duck inside and reach for the blankets.

She pulled one taut to twist into a rope and it tore apart in her hands like tissue. She grabbed another blanket and it turned to dust. She dropped the threads of material with a sob.

The air was too thick and claustrophobia snuck up on her with a sudden intensity and she couldn't fucking stay here anymore. She was nearly halfway out the window before she looked down. Her head spun and the ground telescoped farther away. The fall would kill her. And then the Poppa thing would win. She scrambled back inside.

Nanny's clothes in the closet.

The blankets weren't an option, but maybe the clothing was. One last try. She would tie them together and if it didn't work she would throw herself out the fucking window because she wasn't going to let that thing twist her up anymore. She wouldn't look at it again. It wasn't Poppa and she would go insane if she looked at it again.

She took one last breath of the fresh sweet air and charged across the room, heedless of what lurked in the shadows. She yanked the closet doors open.

CHAPTER 16

THE DOOR DIDN'T lead to the closet anymore. Instead, she stumbled into the tiny bathroom. Her reflection in the mirror was filthy. Her face looked wrinkled. She had never realized how much she looked like Poppa. Everyone always told her she took after her mother's side, but now she saw that she was Poppa through and through. The structure of her face had changed beneath her sallow skin, and she could see his eyes and brow bone protruding through. She looked away when the reflection started to smile.

The air in the bathroom was cool and fresh, much nicer than the air in her room. She felt absurdly grateful for the chance to breathe.

A liquid rush of water trickled into the tub. Her throat clenched. She was so thirsty. She knew she shouldn't eat or drink anything in this wretched apartment, but the thought of water made her throat feel even thicker and drier and she couldn't help herself. She was a deer on shaky legs, making its way towards a spring in the forest.

She knelt before the tub and drank from the faucet. The water was rusty but so good, incredibly good. She gulped it quickly, drinking until her stomach bloated. Only then did she glance into the tub and the pool of water that had accumulated there.

In its reflection, she saw herself. She was nude, her skin porcelain pale, more beautiful than she had ever been in her life. Dead eyes stared blankly, wide open and lifeless. Her mouth hung open in a silent scream. The reflection shimmered, grew. The water ran red and her wrists dangled out of the tub, torn apart in jagged slashes.

She tried to back away but she was frozen in her own gaze.

That giggling again.

With an effort, she tore her eyes free, slid away from the tub. Her injured foot splashed in liquid, and she narrowly avoided another foot full of glass. A bottle lay smashed on the floor, but the red liquid that spilled was too thick to be wine. The shards of glass were wicked daggers, thick and jagged and ready to slice.

The panic was coming again and she didn't know how to stop it. She backed away and her reflection smiled and she was already dead, wasn't she? She looked in her own eyes and they were so angry, but her mouth hung open in a grin. She had succeeded after all.

"You're not me. You're not Poppa and you're not me."

A hot breeze blew papers into the room, tangled threads from the books that had been torn apart. The writing was obscured with blood and the books said *kill yourself cut yourself die die die worthless guilty kill yourself die*

And the air was thick and she felt so tired that she sank to her knees. The image disappeared and the tub

LIKE JAGGED TEETH

was full of water again and the water *drip-drip-dripped* and she was tired and she wanted to sleep. She was ready to sleep forever.

Her fingers twitched with pain and her eyes blinked open. Her hands had a life of their own, toying with glass, nicking small cuts on fingertips. She didn't know how it got there but it was sharp and her skin was so soft and she remembered.

CHAPTER 17

SHE WAS SO TIRED. *Nothing helped. Nothing changed. Junior high was impossible to navigate and she was so fucking sick of being alone. Of being hated. Of not being enough. She was sick of being this stupid dull ugly thing and she had made it worse.*

Black lipstick and heavy eyeliner were not cool or edgy in this small town. They were wrong and scary and got her treated like shit. Instead of spending after school hours with friends she spent them picking spitballs out of her hair and crying raccoon eyes.

The witchcraft book didn't have anything for this exact situation, but she tried to make it work with correspondences and candle magic and whispered hopes and half-uttered prayers. But it didn't work and so she prayed harder, wrote sigils in sketchbooks and it didn't fucking work and they found her sweet little book of shadows and she had made it so much worse.

She was an outcast and she was ridiculous and none of it fucking worked.

There must be something she could do right.

She had cut herself before and liked it. Or liked how it made her feel. Like she was in control of something at least. Wearing the scars of her feelings rather than keeping them bottled up inside. Well, this would be the same, wouldn't it?

She peeled off her shirt and pants. Stripped of her underwear, exposing pale flabby skin. Last of all, she yanked off the pouch she had made, tossed it to the floor. Salt and herbs spilled out. Pathetic.

The bathwater was warm, not hot, it never got hot here. The phone rang somewhere in the distance but she ignored it. She peeled the guard off the razor. There was a ritual to everything, wasn't there?

She was scared and she hated being scared. Wrists shone up at her, translucent in the yellow light. She shouldn't feel like this. She shouldn't feel so scared, heart beating so hard so fast, she should be calm. Sadness was calm and quiet, not afraid.

The water was cold by the time she was ready to cut. The razor opened skin so soft, so easy, it took a few seconds for it to hurt. Through eyes blurred with tears she watched the water swirl with Rorschach splotches of deep dark red until even those were gone and she sat in a stinking pool of her own blood.

How long would it take? Why did she still feel so afraid? She thought she would go calm and quiet and sleepy and dead but her heart kept beating fast and hard as it pumped out spurts of blood.

Please, please go to sleep. Please. So tired.

The phone rang again, a scream in the night.

And now she was finally getting sleepy and she closed her eyes and time passed and somewhere far away she heard the door slam and Poppa was yelling and he came up the stairs and she hadn't locked the door. He knew somehow, of course, he always knew and why hadn't she locked the door?

BETTY ROCKSTEADY

She had almost made it and then Poppa was there with sirens in the distance. It was freezing outside the tub and that woke her up and she lay on the hard floor, frozen and naked and Poppa pressed bright white towels to her wrists and she hadn't cut deep enough, not really, had she?

The sirens were here and she was saved and Poppa held her close, his eyes brown and so, so sad and as the EMTs pounded up the staircase he whispered in her ear, "You're strong, little girl. Don't let the bad guys win."

CHAPTER 18

JACALYN DIDN'T WANT to let the bad guys win. The glass dropped from her hands. From outside the room, something howled. The face in the tub leered, but it wasn't her. Not anymore. But what could she do? She was so fucking tired, still, forever. She didn't know how to fight. She didn't know how to save herself. She had been carrying around too many awful feelings for too long. Too much guilt, wrapped tight around her like a cloak, and that was what this thing wanted, wasn't it? Poppa would never have wanted that for her. Poppa wasn't this awful diseased thing— he had been happy and strong and she had made a mistake and she was sorry and he would forgive her. Wouldn't he? Hadn't she been through enough?

She didn't know what the hell that thing was but she had to try to fight it.

She left the bathroom and the pale girl in the tub behind. Yellow wallpaper peeled from the walls and slithered across the floor. The window streamed open, enticing, but the fall was too much and she just needed to think. The air was refreshing at least, and she curled up onto the bed and watched the wallpaper stir and the papers dance in the breeze.

Slugs crept across the walls, leaving thick trails of

slime. Ugly voices called to her from the hallway. *Are you ready to apologize?* She didn't answer. Distorted faces peered at her from corners and she felt numb.

Even her own body wasn't safe. The dust from the walls covered her and she faded. Her skin grew dry, mummified, flaked away. She ached deep inside. Black blood stained the blanket beneath her and she stank of piss and sweat and her flesh turned red and bubbled, necrotic.

She covered her eyes. The noises grew louder. The walls wept and screams echoed just beyond the windows. She covered her ears and something nipped at her eyes, begging her to look. It was impossible to think in here. Time warped and burbled and became indistinct. The room wavered and she wavered within it. There were no answers, not here. There was nothing but time. The walls grew larger and smaller, darker and brighter with the light of the red moon washing through.

Insects crept out of the walls. Sleepy-eyed, Jacalyn watched them slink across the floor. Fat thick spiders lingered in the shadows, springing upon millipedes that ran too fast and they all ate each other and their tiny thin shrieks lulled her to sleep.

The air was thick enough to taste, like mildew.

She hadn't felt like herself in a long time.

The wallpaper changed when she blinked. Patterns of pale yellow and mustard danced and she could see someone peering back out at her, someone creeping and slinking along the walls.

Nothing was right in here but she would remain calm. She swallowed her fear. She felt nothing. Her sleepy mind wanted to believe that she was being brave, but she was being lulled along a sick pathway and the closet door gaped open and she could hear the faucet *drip-drip-drip* but she didn't care. She would sit here in vigilance on the bed. She would just sit here.

The insects carried notes to her, scraps of paper that had been mutated and changed and they said *it's your fault everything is your fault* and so she closed her eyes.

A mass fell from the ceiling, cool and sizzling, and landed on her poor aching foot. She didn't want to look, she couldn't look, just brushed it away and it stung but she wouldn't look anymore.

Are you ready to apologize, you little bitch? Don't you feel awful for what you've done? The voice came from somewhere inside her head.

She kept her eyes shut tight. She remembered when she believed in something beyond herself but now she was all alone. This place was wrong and if she couldn't get out she would just shut down. She would ignore it. She would escape inside herself.

The sounds that came from the hallway were not there. She concentrated on her breathing. She shut her eyes, she held her hands over her ears and she would remain calm, she would remain calm.

The panic in her chest was far away. The bugs that crawled over her skin were farther. The thing on her foot that bubbled and sucked was not there at all. The bathroom didn't exist. The rustling paper and the messages were not for her and she kept her eyes shut and she blocked it out and she would not listen she would not listen and days or months or seconds passed and she transcended.

CHAPTER 19

THEY WERE SITTING on the swing in Poppa's backyard. It was an old people's swing. You couldn't go high, but you could sit together and rock back and forth. She never sat there on her own, it was too boring, but sometimes Poppa would read to her out here and that was nice.

He wasn't reading to her today. Today he sat next to her and held her hand. He shifted his weight and they swayed. She swung her feet.

"It wants to control you, Jacalyn. It controls you by your guilt. It eats it up. Don't let it. You're smart and you're strong. You don't have to let it." She looked up at her Poppa and his eyes were kind and his own.

"I don't know how to stop it." She was too small. Her legs didn't even touch the ground as they swung. "I think it's too late. I'm really tired."

Poppa sighed and handed her a glass. "Have something to drink, sweetie. You have to keep your strength up."

Jacalyn held the glass with both hands and put it up to her lips. She kept her eyes on Poppa. Something wasn't right. It was him, but the shadows that swirled behind him were black and threatening as thunderclouds. The sky was going dark too fast.

LIKE JAGGED TEETH

"Hurry." There was fear in his eyes. "I'm afraid there's not much time."

Jacalyn drank and there was no water, there was no liquid at all. Her mouth filled with salt. She looked at Poppa, confused, but Poppa wasn't there anymore, something else was, and its flesh turned black and peeled back and she was screaming again. She dropped the glass and salt spilled everywhere and something small in the back of her brain woke up.

CHAPTER 20

JACALYN WOKE UP, TOO. Something tickled her face. She brushed it away, and a fat centipede clung to her hand, tiny legs scrabbling for purchase. She grimaced and flicked it away. It splattered against the wall with a soft plop, leaving a thin thread of mucous behind.

The room was a disaster. While she slept it had further corrupted. The veneer of normality was gone, disintegrated, replaced by rot and mold. Maggots crawled across the carpet in a line, piggybacking their way across the room. Wallpaper peeled back to reveal singed wood. This would not be a safe place much longer. The floor was coated in diseased-looking fluids. It was time to do something.

From the hallway, wet squelching noises. Something eating from a trough.

Her nightgown was tight against her sweaty skin. There was a sheen of grease across her entire body. Everything was filthy. She was unclean. Unwholesome.

Her stomach growled. It was sick the way her body kept going, kept *needing* even in a situation like this. She didn't want to walk across the filthy floor, but she had to. It was time to go. It was time to move.

LIKE JAGGED TEETH

Jacalyn took a deep, shaky breath. *Fake it 'til you make it.* Poppa had told her that once, so so long ago.

"Poppa?" she called.

The room groaned, contracted. The breeze from the window was icy cold, but the air remained stale. Stagnant. Jacalyn was dry as a desert. She was weak and sick and her foot hurt and she couldn't stay in here any longer.

"Poppa. I don't feel well. I'm sorry for what I said . . . can you please come help me?" The floor was too dangerous to step on, full of glass and insects and filth.

She heard footsteps in the hallway. Too many footsteps. They clattered through the empty hall. He didn't answer but she could feel him standing there, outside the door. Waiting.

A spider climbed up the lamp, weaving a thin strand of web. It was as large as her palm, and as she watched, it snagged a maggot the size of her thumb and sank fangs into it with a wet squelch. She shuddered. It crouched, watching her. The wallpaper shifted.

"Poppa, I'm sorry!" She tried to interject more feeling into her voice. Sincerity. It was hard. Her throat was so dry, so raspy. Her stomach was sick. She pulled her foot up to examine it, keeping the spider in her peripheral vision.

Her foot was a ruin. The pain had been reduced to a dull aching, distant, numb; but that was worrisome too. Her entire foot was a dusky grey color. Dead looking. The place where the glass had ripped the flesh open was swollen and red as blood, with necrotic-looking black tissue all around it. Snakes of dark blue and red surged up her calf. She wasn't sure she would be able to stand on it.

Raspy breath came from the other side of the door. Would she die in here? Without food or water? How long had it been since she had eaten or drank anything? The room closed in further. She stank. She was afraid to stand. She was afraid.

"POPPA," she cried. Her voice cracked. She needed it to answer her. Desperation bubbled in the pit of her stomach and finally she heard its voice.

It was dark and raspy and layered with a multitude of sickening tones. "Have you learned your lesson, then?" Oily shadows slipped through the crack beneath the door.

"Yes," she screamed. She felt near hysterical. More bugs circled the bed. Hornets had joined now, and they were large, their stingers razor sharp and vile looking. "Yes, I'm sorry!"

"Sorry for what?" it urged, its voice oily. "What do you say?"

Jacalyn breathed in and tried to remain still. The insects eyed her. She could smell her own stink. She thought of the years she had avoided her grandparents. She thought of how she had stolen from her Poppa, who would have given her the shirt off his back. She thought of how unappreciative she had been. Of the times he had tried to tell her stories and she had only half-listened, waiting to go do something more exciting. She thought of what she had done. All of that trembled in her voice and she said, "I'm sorry I said you weren't my Poppa. I'm so sorry. I love you so much."

The door swung open. The thing stood there. Its eyes were black. Its shoulders were stooped. Its arms were too long, slender fingers tapering towards the floor. Its head brushed the ceiling and its smile spread beyond its cheeks. "I love you, too, Jacalyn." And it opened its arms.

Light spilled in from the hallway. The bugs scattered and the breeze blew the glass and papers out of her way. A path was clear. Jacalyn stepped tentatively from the bed and hobbled across the room on her shaky feet, into his arms.

CHAPTER 21

POPPA LED HER into the hallway, supporting her with both arms. She hung heavily from him, shifting as much weight off her foot as she could.

"You've been in there a long time," Poppa said. He walked quicker than she could keep up, dragging her along. "You must be starving." The kitchen stank. The same rotten meat sat on the table, swarming with flies. Jacalyn was horrified to hear her stomach gurgle in anticipation of getting fed. The table was set with salt and pepper shakers and a tall glass of water. Drops of condensation formed on the glass, making her mouth water. She was famished, but she couldn't eat that. She wouldn't.

"Thanks for making a meal, Poppa," she said, carefully, "but I'd really like to go to the bathroom first, if I could." She was afraid to look into his eyes. "I need to get washed up. I'm . . . I haven't bathed in days."

"You don't need to worry about that stuff anymore. It's just me and you here. Forever. You have no one to impress." Poppa nodded toward the table. "Sit. Eat."

The meat beckoned. It was wet and misshapen. Jacalyn tore her eyes away from the table, with effort.

LIKE JAGGED TEETH

"Well, I really need to pee at least. And wash my hands." She held them out so Poppa could see. They were covered with filth and spattered with blood, she could only assume from her foot. A wrinkle of a frown appeared on Poppa's forehead. "You always make me wash my hands before dinner," she added quickly. The wrinkle smoothed out, but something nasty sparkled in his eyes.

"That's right. Good girl. Well, I'll just have to help you." His smile slanted.

"I can do it myself." It was hard to look at him. His face kept changing. The features of her grandfather melted away, exposing muscle and tendon. He stormed into the hall and ripped a door open.

Jacalyn's stomach turned. What if it was that awful tiny bathroom again? But the door swung in and it was the first bathroom again, the one with the toilet and the filthy shower.

"Thanks, Poppa. I can take it from here." Jacalyn hobbled towards the toilet.

"Nonsense. You're absolutely filthy. I'll help you into the shower."

She had stayed calm throughout all of this, god, she was trying so hard to stay calm, but his voice set off a tinny feeling of fear again. "No, no, that's all right, I'll just wash up in the sink. It's fine." She was playing a very dangerous game. His reflection grinned at her from the mirror above the sink. His jaw unhinged slowly, a pinkish thread of drool extending from his lips. Her own face was unfamiliar, pale and blank.

"Hygiene is important." His voice was deep and husky. Jacalyn froze. He slinked behind her, a blur of shadow. She watched her own eyes widen in horror, as he pressed against her with a groan. Pallid, strange hands reached around to undo the buttons, one at a time. She was unable to move or struggle. She stood completely still as he pulled the pajama gown off her shoulders.

Her nude form was thinner than it had been in years. It was pale and prepubescent and she shook as the skeletal thumbs hooked into the elastic waistband of her underwear.

"You've grown into a lovely young woman." He pressed against her bottom, and a flurry of butterflies flapped wings in her chest.

"Will you draw the bath for me?" A tear trickled down her cheek. "With bubbles? Like you used to?"

The thing pulled away from her with a chuckle. It walked to the bath, leaving her standing alone, cold and vulnerable.

It settled on knees with too many joints, slender arms navigated into the tub.

It turned its back on her.

Quickly, quickly, Jacalyn yanked the heavy lid off the toilet tank. Her arms were thin as twigs, barely strong enough to hold it, but they did, and when the thing turned, she threw the weight of her entire body into it, swung it like a baseball bat and smashed it into the horrible thing's face.

When her Poppa had fallen down the stairs, he made the most horrible noise she had ever heard and this sound was the same but different somehow. Triumphant. And she didn't stop, she couldn't stop, she smashed the lid into it again and again until the ceramic broke and its skull broke and all that was left on his shoulders was mush and broken bits of bone. It was impossible to tell what was part of the lid and what was part of him and she didn't have time to cry or to get dressed, she had to run, she had to get out of here *now*.

She slid out the door, running into the kitchen, but she had to turn back, she needed the key and she patted him down, reached into his shirt pocket and the key was there, on the keychain she had given him when she was little—*World's Greatest Grandpa*—and she was crying freely now but she ran, her bare feet slippery on the tile floor and she nearly slid and crashed into the apartment door but she was free now and she would get out.

She jammed the key into the keyhole. There was a moment where she knew, just knew that the door would never open and she would be trapped in here with the rotting thing forever but the door swung open and behind it was another door. A dark door lay beyond this one and her hands were on the doorknob and she spun it and it opened and there was another door and she was hysterical and there was another door and another and there was no escape and she heard something moving behind her.

CHAPTER 22

SHE COULDN'T SEE IT, but she could hear it, a wet slurping sound as it peeled itself from the floor. It wasn't dead, not yet, and how could you kill something that was already dead? A flutter of panic rolled in her stomach. There was no escape. It had to be the window then. And if she fell to her death, smashed head and limbs against concrete, so be it. Being dead was better than being trapped here. Better than looking into the eyes of that awful thing even one more time.

"Jacalyn . . . " her name was garbled. He didn't have much face left to speak from, but that didn't stop him. She struggled to keep her breaths even and calm. She had to keep calm. The kitchen shimmered and warped around her, dark pus dripping from the ceiling. A chattering sound came from the walls. She had to get to her room before he—*it*—pulled itself up from the bathroom floor and came after her. "Jacalyn, where are you?" He didn't sound like her Poppa, not at all.

She lurched forward on her aching foot. Light glinted on the canister of salt that sat on the table and she grabbed it. She shuffled painfully into the hallway.

"Jacalyn, come help your Poppa up. Why did you

hit me like that? Oh, it hurts. I need your help." Tears came to her eyes but she brushed them aside. Beneath his voice, something bubbled and twisted. She knew it wasn't him, but fear and guilt twisted together and she felt like she had been bad.

She couldn't face him. She wouldn't look. The doors were all mixed up. She couldn't remember which one led where but the bathroom was at the end of the hall and she could see it moving and shifting in her periphery. She tried the door nearest to her, but the doorknob was shut so tight it twisted her wrist painfully.

"Come help your Poppa, you little bitch," it growled. More wet noises as he squirmed forward. She turned to the next doorknob and she saw him, couldn't help herself.

His face was inflating back up, slowly. Red wet meat sat atop his shoulders, dripping to the floor in wet plops. Burst eyes rose on stalks, blind but seeking her out. There was a rasping sound as the palps that stuck of out his neck drew in air, sputtering out blood and something thick and black. With each raspy breath, the muscle and tendon rebuilt a bit more as he drew himself back together. "Why would you hurt your Poppa like this? Oh, you're in a world of trouble now, little girl."

"You're not my Poppa!"

Horror made her breath shallow and she turned the next knob and it was the awful bathroom and she would not look into her own dead pale face again and she turned around to the next door and his breath was hot on her neck and his bony hands raked her shoulders but the door opened and she fell inside.

Her room was dim and bare. Everything was

falling apart. The bugs had left. The books were gone. The floor was clean and bare. Jacalyn tried to catch her breath. The Poppa thing pounded on the door and she pushed it shut tightly with her back.

He cackled, "Little pig, little pig, let me in."

The window was too far. The room tunneled away from her, dusky and grey. It was not her room. Nothing here was hers. She couldn't escape, not even through the window. By the time she made it there, he would burst in and be upon her and . . . god knows what he would do then. Even if she made it to the window all that waited for her outside was broken bones. A retched sob escaped her throat. Was there no escape then?

She was so fucking tired.

"I'll blow this door down!" He screeched, and Jacalyn shook as he pounded his fists against the door. "This is my house, and my fucking rules, Jacalyn! You can't hide from me!"

She looked into her hand at the pillar of salt. Foggily, she remembered her dream. *Salt is for protection*. Wisps of paper blew by, memories of books she had read and things she had learned.

It had never worked before. Nothing ever worked. A thin thread of hope unfurled in her, though, a feeling she barely recognized. What else was left?

The Poppa thing pounded harder. The door shook. The walls shook. Jacalyn's shoulders shook, uncontrollably.

The top of the salt pillar unscrewed easily. Could she remember? Her brain was muddy and unsure. It had been so long. It was mostly about belief. It was all about belief. The pain circled within her, a deadly soup within her gut, but she had to push it aside. She brought up his face in her mind, his real face, not the mask this fucking thing wore.

She would cast a circle then. She stepped away from the door. It wouldn't hold for long.

There wasn't a lot of salt. It trickled between her fingers, made such a small pile in her palm. She sat on the floor, facing the door, facing the thing head on. Her eyes watered. Her skin was dry and cracked. She had cried so much lately. She spread the salt around her, pinching it between fingers. She didn't know what to say. She had been a witch once, or thought she had been, when she was in her early teens. She had cast spells to turn the bullies aside, but they had never worked.

Grains of salt stuck to her fingers. She tried to picture a warm light emanating from them, but dark shapes writhed in the corners of the room and it was so hard to ignore them, to ignore the sounds coming from the other side of the door. She inhaled and exhaled deeply, but her breath came ragged and uneven. She was trying, oh god, she was trying. "With this sacred salt, I cast a circle . . . to protect me from . . . from . . . " She didn't know what to say.

"I'm coming, Jacalyn." The voice didn't sound like her grandfather at all anymore. It didn't sound human. "I'll eat your heart and I'll shit it out and put it back inside you and then you'll listen, you'll have to listen. Then we can start all over again." He pounded against the door and it splintered and cracked.

She looked at her salt circle in despair. It was nothing. It was pathetic. The grains of salt were like sand and he would thrust his way through the door and have his way with her and her pathetic attempt at protection would be scattered in the wind like so much dust and she should have gone for the window after all.

The door splintered and cracked and she saw his rotten face poking through. He licked the splinters with a long slimy tongue, sending drops of black blood dripping to the floor. His dead dark eyes were full of teeth and they gnashed at her, ready to eat. She didn't want it to see her cry but she couldn't help it and tears leaked from her cheeks, spilling onto the salt, and it broke through.

CHAPTER 23

"**PLEASE.**"

Through the broken shards of the door, the features of her grandfather were blurred into mush. The face was so distorted, it could never be recognized as human. It was so hard to look at it, it kept changing, a swirl of insanity. "It's all your fault. You've ruined everything, you little shit. You've got to be punished. You have to get what you deserve. You let me down. You fucking murdered me!"

She shut her eyes tight, shook her head. She couldn't look at this awful thing anymore. With her eyes shut, the voice didn't sound like Poppa's at all. It sounded like something deep within the earth, awful and crunching and ripping.

She heard the door torn apart. She curled into herself. She was so weak and thin and shallow. She couldn't do this anymore. She couldn't bear another minute of this.

Bits of wood splintered and attacked her bare arms and chest. She couldn't be here anymore. She needed to be somewhere safe. Somewhere secret. She pictured her cubby, her secret place. Her good place. She pictured her Poppa, the real one, his wrinkled face smiling, safe, loving.

"Look at me! LOOK AT WHAT YOU'VE DONE."

She wiped her eyes painfully, dry skin ripping and it was through the door and she couldn't help it, she opened her eyes. He looked like her Poppa again, at that last moment, that worst moment. The beast had shrunk back down to human size and lolled in the splintered door, broken and hesitant, head tilted horribly, limbs shattered and splayed.

"You want to forget, don't you? You can forget again. I'll swallow your memories and we can start all over, how does that sound?"

"I didn't mean to!" Her tears dripped to the floor, fat and glistening, mingling with the salt. Her dead Poppa reached for her, arms expanding, rubbery, and from the clay-like mixture of salt and moisture something moved.

The mixture rose. Grew. Shifted into a tornado of motion, so much salt, so much more than she had thought. The Poppa thing reared back. The tornado twisted toward the ceiling, and the salt reformed in a simulacrum of a person. Her fear and pain washed away, replaced with wonder.

It was Poppa.

The image of her Poppa that the thing had stolen paled in comparison to this simple shape—this *feeling* that was her Poppa, her real Poppa, through and through. His shoulders were broad again, and his hands were powerful. The salt man was crude but felt solid. Felt real.

Love spread from it, filled her heart where the fear had been. Filled her with strength and she couldn't stop crying but it was different now. Her tears powered him and propelled him forward. She was weak and small and sad but he was everything and he radiated forgiveness and light. She choked down the sobs.

She closed her eyes and in the darkness she saw her Poppa, as he really was. Her family. A man who faced challenges head-on. A man who loved her from the moment he saw her, the first moment he held her in his arms. A man who would do anything for his family. And she had made mistakes, but that's all they had been. Mistakes.

"You're not Poppa. Poppa would forgive me." And she released the last of her guilt, finally. "I forgive myself." She opened her eyes.

The Poppa thing roared. It sputtered. It sloughed off the remains of its human form. What lay beneath was sick and sticky, a black tumorous form. With a strangled cry it lurched forward, reaching for Jacalyn, but as it touched the salt it sizzled. The scent of rotten meat filled the room. Globs of flesh dripped down the flannel it wore. Eyeballs bulged and withered and begged. Teeth crumbled and fell and turned to dust. She watched, her heart full of forgiveness and love.

The flannel dissolved and revealed scrawny tendon and gristle. The salt picked away at it, disintegrating painful wisps of flesh, until all that was left was a faint black smudge where the thing had been. Jacalyn blew out a breath and it collapsed, and all that was left was a pile of dirty salt.

"Poppa?" The room was silent. She didn't feel him there anymore, but she felt him inside her. There was room for him now, without all that awful black guilt clouding up the way. The remnants of her guilt sizzled into the floor, thick and black and sticky, leaving holes in the wood. She stirred the salt gently with her fingertip.

BETTY ROCKSTEADY

The walls were crumbling. The ground beneath her shook. A scent like burning. There was nothing for her here. Not now, not ever. She pulled herself to her feet, walked through the hall as quickly as she could, mindful of her sore foot. The apartment creaked and crumbled around her, wallpaper turning to dust, fixtures turning to piles of bugs and slime.

The front door opened easily now and led out to bright fresh air. The apartment was falling apart fast and there wasn't much time to get out, but she looked back and said, "Thank you, Poppa. I love you."

And finally, she walked outside.

CHAPTER 24

THE SUN WAS coming up over the horizon, illuminating the red and orange leaves that had fallen from the trees. Time had passed, but how much? She wasn't far from home. The air was cold on her bare skin. She stumbled home, barefoot and pained and anxious.

She drew a few curious stares, but she made it. The key was under the doorstop, where it had always been. She let herself inside.

She had been crying a lot lately, and she couldn't stop even now. A fierce gratitude struck her. Her home was plush and comfortable and everyone was still asleep. She was filthy and her foot would need attention sooner rather than later, but she had something she wanted to do first.

She stumbled to the room where her grandmother lay. She held her breath for a moment, hoping against hope that it wasn't too late. But there she was. Slumber made her look younger than she was, smoothed out the wrinkles of her face. Jacalyn sat in the chair next to her, exhausted, and took her small, frail hand in her own. Nanny barely stirred, but a smile teased at the corner of her mouth.

Through the crack of the curtains, she watched as

the sun rose. Soon her mother would arise, and there would be some explaining to do. And hot showers. And good food. And medical attention. But for now, she would just hold her Nanny's hand and enjoy the feeling of home and forgiveness around her.

ABOUT THE AUTHOR

Betty Rocksteady is your everyday Canadian weirdo with a leaning towards the macabre and grotesque. Besides writing violent and sexual and just plain weird fiction, she does black and white horror illustration. Her debut novella, *Arachnophile*, was part of Eraserhead Press' 2015 New Bizarro Authors Series. If you've been dying to read about a man who falls in love with a giant spider, this is probably the book for you. Her short fiction has been published in *Eternal Frankenstein, Lost Signals, Turn to Ash,* and *DOA III*. Find out more at www.bettyrocksteady.com or connect on twitter @bettyrocksteady.

IF YOU ENJOYED
LIKE JAGGED TEETH
DON'T PASS UP ON THESE OTHER TITLES
FROM PERPETUAL MOTION MACHINE . . .

THE TRAIN DERAILS IN BOSTON

BY JESSICA MCHUGH

ISBN: 978-1-943720-06-4
Page count: 346
$14.95

Rebecca Malone has problems. Not just the alcohol. Not just her husband's inane attempts at writing a bestselling novel, their teenage daughter's promiscuity, or her certifiable mother. Not even her lover, who wants to take her husband's place in Cherrywood Lodge, the famous estate she now calls home. Her biggest issues start the moment she discovers a chest of ancient mahjong tiles in the basement of her new house, causing her life to spin out of control with hallucinations, sexual deviances, and grisly murders. Is the mahjong game haunted? Or are Rebecca's problems part of a different game, started before she was born?

FOUR DAYS
BY ELI WILDE AND 'ANNA DEVINE

ISBN: 978-0-9887488-5-9

Page count: 190

$9.95

Weirdos were always attracted to Emily Cullen. There had always been an allure. Freakish moths drawn to some kind of light she oozed. From an early age it was a light she wished she could switch off. The monster was different. He was weird, but he was also insanely bold. His attraction to Emily was boundless, just like his love for her. Love fuelled by psychopathic tendencies and meth head mentality.

He had planned the abduction meticulously, right down to the clothes she would wear, the pornography she would watch and the rules she would obey. Emily knew something bad was about to happen, but her friends and family didn't believe her. Just like they never believed her when she told them about the dead people she saw, the ones attracted to her since she first came into this world.

THE VIOLATORS
BY VINCENZO BILOF

ISBN: 978-1-943720-02-6
Page count: 260
$14.95

Alan Chambers, an anxious loser whose goal is to become a prominent English professor, has just been accepted into the exclusive class on The Artistry of Contemporary Literature. His excitement is dampened when he learns that his new classmates are dedicated to human violation in the name of art. They have given Alan one responsibility—destroy them.

These literary violators have discovered a primal link between literature, art, sexuality, and murder. But rape and kidnapping as a means to analyze the works of James Joyce and Homer have lost their allure, and only Alan can save them from themselves.

A novel that transcends genre tropes while serving as a satirical commentary on contemporary fiction, David Lynch meets William S. Burroughs in this lucid postmodern nightmare.

The Perpetual Motion Machine Catalog

Bleed | Various Authors | Anthology
    Page count: 286 | Paperback: $16.95
    ISBN: 978-0-9887488-8-0

Crabtown, USA:Essays & Observations |
    Rafael Alvarez | Essays
    Page count: 466 | Paperback: $16.95
    ISBN: 978-1-943720-03-3

Cruel | Eli Wilde | Novel
    Page count: 192 | Paperback: $9.95
    ISBN: 978-0-9887488-0-4

Dead Men | John Foster | Novel
    Page Count: 360 | Paperback: $16.95
    ISBN: 978-0-9860594-7-6

Destroying the Tangible Issue of Reality; or, Searching
    for Andy Kaufmann | T. Fox Dunham | Novel
    Page Count: 430 | Paperback: $14.95
    ISBN: 978-0-9860594-2-1

Four Days | Eli Wilde & 'Anna DeVine | Novel
    Page count: 198 | Paperback: $9.95
    ISBN: 978-0-9887488-5-9

Gory Hole | Craig Wallwork | Story Collection (Full-
    Color Illustrations)
    Page count: 48 | Paperback: $12.95
    ISBN: 978-0-9860594-3-8

The Green Kangaroos | Jessica McHugh | Novel
  Page count: 184 | Paperback $12.95
  ISBN: 978-0-9860594-6-9

Invasion of the Weirdos | Andrew Hilbert | Novel
  Page count: 242 | Paperback $16.95
  ISBN: 978-1-943720-20-0

Last Dance in Phoenix | Kurt Reichenbaugh | Novel
  Page count: 268 | Paperback: $12.95
  ISBN: 978-0-9860594-9-0

Long Distance Drunks: a Tribute to Charles Bukowski Various Authors | Anthology
  Page count: 182 | Paperback: $12.95
  ISBN: 978-0-9860594-4-5

Lost Signals | Various Authors | Anthology
  Page count: 378 | Paperback: $16.95
  ISBN: 978-1-943720-08-8

Mojo Rising | Bob Pastorella | Novella
  Page count: 142 | Paperback $9.95
  ISBN: 978-1-943720-05-7

The Perpetual Motion Club | Sue Lange | Novel
  Page count: 208 | Paperback $14.95
  ISBN: 978-0-9887488-6-6

The Ritalin Orgy | Matthew Dexter | Novel
  Page count: 206 | Paperback $12.95
  ISBN: 978-0-9887488-1-1

The Ruin Season | Kristopher Triana | Novel
  Page count: 324 | Paperback $14.95
  ISBN: 978-1-943720-07-1

Sirens | Kurt Reichenbaugh | Novel
Page count: 286 | Paperback: $14.95
ISBN: 978-0-9887488-3-5

So it Goes: a Tribute to Kurt Vonnegut | Various
Authors Anthology
Page count: 282 | Paperback $14.95
ISBN: 978-0-9887488-2-8

Tales from the Holy Land | Rafael Alvarez |
Story Collection
Page count: 226 | Paperback $12.95
ISBN: 978-0-9860594-0-7

The Tears of Isis | James Dorr | Story Collection
Page count: 206 | Paperback: $12.95
ISBN: 978-0-9887488-4-2

The Train Derails in Boston | Jessica McHugh | Novel
Page count: 346 | Paperback: $14.95
ISBN: 978-1-943720-06-4

The Violators | Vincenzo Bilof | Novel
Page Count: 260 | Paperback: $14.95
ISBN: 978-1-943720-02-6

Time Eaters | Jay Wilburn | Novel
Page count: 218 | Paperback: $12.95
ISBN: 978-0-9887488-7-3

Vampire Strippers from Saturn | Vincenzo Bilof | Novel
Page count: 210 | Paperback: $12.95
ISBN: 978-0-9860594-8-3

Patreon:
www.patreon.com/PMMPublishing

Website:
www.PerpetualPublishing.com

Facebook:
www.facebook.com/PerpetualPublishing

Twitter:
@PMMPublishing

Instagram:
www.instagram.com/PMMPublishing

Newsletter:
www.PMMPNews.com

Email Us:
Contact@PerpetualPublishing.com

CPSIA information can be obtained
at www.ICGtesting.com
Printed in the USA
LVHW05s2127260918
591493LV00001B/34/P

9 781943 720217